Improvisation, Theatre Games and Scene Handbook

Courtesy of the William-Alan Landes collection from Columbia Pictures, 1938, the film version of Philip Barry's *HOLIDAY*. Sisters Julia (Dorris Nolan) and Linda (Katharine Hepburn) seem to have one man in mind: Johnny.

PLAYERS PRESS PERFORMANCE WORKSHOP

Improvisation, Theatre Games and Scene Handbook

by

Samuel Elkind

PLAYERS PRESS, Inc.
P.O. Box 1132
Studio City, California 91614
U.S.A.

A.C.T.
AUSTRALIA

Essex
UNITED KINGDOM

IMPROVISATION, THEATRE GAMES AND SCENE HANDBOOK

ISBN 0-88734-940-4

Editorial: William-Alan Landes and Chris Cordero
Typeset and Design Layout: Chris Cordero
Paste-Up: Chris Cordero

Simultaneously Published
U.S.A., U.K., Canada and Australia
Printed in the U.S.A.

Library of Congress Cataloging-in-Publication Data

Elkind, Samuel.
Improvisation, theatre games and scene handbook / by Samuel Elkind.
p. cm. -- (Players Press performance workshop)
ISBN 0-88734-940-4 (alk. paper)
1. Improvisation (Acting) 2. Acting. 3. Drama--Collections. I. Title. II. Series.

PN2071.I5 E43 2003
792'.082--dc21

2002032752

ACKNOWLEDGMENTS

ANGEL STREET by Patrick Hamilton. Copyright 1939 by Patrick Hamilton. Under the title, Gaslight. Copyright renewed 1967 by Ursula Winifred Hamilton. Reprinted by permission of A.M. Health & Company Ltd., agents for the estate of the late Patrick Hamilton.

"Going to Pot" by Georges Feydeau, translated by Norman R. Shapiro. Abridgement of the Play "Going to Pot" from the book FOUR FACES by Georges Feydeau, translated by Norman R. Shapiro. 1959, 1961, 1962 and 1970 by Norman R. Shapiro. Reprinted by permission of The University of Chicago Press and Norman R. Shapiro.

HOLIDAY by Philip Barry. Copyright, 1928, by Philip Barry. Copyright, 1929, by Philip Barry. Copyright, 1955 (In Renewal), by Ellen S. Barry. Copyright, 1956 (In Renewal), by Ellen S. Barry.
CAUTION: Professionals and amateurs are hereby warned that "Holiday", being fully protected under the Copyright Laws of the United States of America, the British Commonwealth, including the Dominion of Canada, and all other countries of the Copyright Union, the Berne Convention, the Pan-American Copyright Convention and the Universal Copyright Convention, are subject to license and royalty. All rights including, but not limited to, reproduction in whole or in part by any process or method, professional use, amateur use, film, recitation, lecturing, public reading, recording, taping, radio casting, and the rights of translation into foreign languages, are strictly reserved. Royalties must be paid to Samuel French, Inc., at 25 West 45th Street, New York, NY 10036 or 7623 Sunset Blvd., Hollywood, California, or if Canada to Samuel French (Canada), Ltd., at 27 Grenville Street., Toronto, Ont.

J.B. by Archibald MacLeish. © Copyright, 1956, 1957, 1958 by Archibald MacLeish. Reprinted by permission of the publisher, Houghton Mifflin Company. All rights reserved. All inquiries concerning stock and amateur acting rights should be addressed to Samuel French, Inc., 25 West 45th Street, New York, New York 10036.
CAUTION: Professionals and amateurs are hereby warned that "J.B.", being fully protected under the Copyright Laws of the United States of America, the British Commonwealth, including the Dominion of Canada, and all other countries of the Copyright Union, the Berne Convention, the Pan-American Copyright Convention and the Universal Copyright Convention, are subject to license and royalty. All rights including, but not limited to, reproduction in whole or in part by any process or method, professional use, amateur use, film, recitation, lecturing, public reading, recording, taping, radio casting, and the rights of translation into foreign languages, are strictly reserved. Particular

PHOTOS

Courtesy of Columbia Pictures. Johnny (Cary Grant) and Linda (Katharine Hepburn) playing at life, from the 1938 film version of Philip Barry's play *HOLIDAY*.

CONTENTS

3 A Resource Book page 84

4 Scenes for Practice page 113

PUBLISHER'S DEDICATION

I have known Dr. Samuel Elkind close to three decades and known of him for over forty years. Sam had a productive and illustrious career in the professional and educational theatre worlds. He has received numerous acknowledgments, awards and honors from his peers. He was a family man and an outstanding contributor to his community. It was a great loss when he passed away.

I met Sam when I was a kid acting in New York, again when I was working and studying theatre in London, and in Los Angeles when I was changing focus from television and film as an actor to directing and producing. At each stage, Sam added much to my career with his suggestions, advice and criticism. I was pleased to have known him and proud to have called him a friend.

But the highlight of our relationship came in the late 1980's, when I was producing and directing for Merrick Studios. Sam asked me about publishing four books he had. He knew that I was a contributor for Showcase Magazine and on the board of directors for Players Press; I suggested he send his books to the company and see what happened. He did and I was surprised when I was asked to be the editor. I was delighted when I looked at the first book in the series, *Scenes for Acting and Directing, Volume 1.* It was something we really needed — scene cuttings from professional plays with director's notes.

Sam was delighted I accepted the job of editor for his books, which later became a source of friction between us. I edited Volumes 1 and 2 and they were published, received well and very successful. They are still used by more schools, actors, and directors than any scene books I know of, including my own.

I had an accident which limited my work as an actor-director. At the same time, the publishing company was looking for a publisher. It was a marriage made in heaven — or at least on stage. But the change from occasional editor to publisher brought heavy demands on my time. As much as I wanted to see Sam's last two books published, and as great as the demand for them was, I couldn't get to finish them. He was understanding, but by the time eight years had passed he was disappointed. I remember his telephone call to me on his return from London; we joked and he asked if I'd ever get finished with books 3 and 4. I promised I would, and they were both scheduled for 2003.

Both books got published this year. Unfortunately, Sam died. I'm sorry he's not here to see his work in print, but I know thousands of actors, directors, teachers and students will appreciate Sam's work. Thank you, Sam.

William-Alan Landes
Publisher

INTRODUCTION

The well-trained actor has at his command a variety of improvisational skills. To develop these skills the actor will have participated in theatre games, knowing that "games" are played for the purpose of exploring and/or dealing with acting problems—the fundamentals of improvisation are the same as those of a game.

A theatre game is a group effort—a corporate aesthetic enterprise with certain agreed upon limitations or guidelines. While a game generally may be fun and a pleasant experience, understanding the purpose of the game makes the activity even more rewarding.

A game also depends on individuality; that is, each player's uniqueness, his/her personal style of playing the game. Each player's imagination and spontaneous reactions add to the game, keep it moving and changing quickly. The course and outcome of the game are unplanned and unpredictable, for no player can be entirely sure what any other will say or do next. Thus, each game reaches its conclusion in a way different from all previous games. Individual spontaneity is the element of surprise which holds everyone's interest, whether one is a player or an observer.

Playing a game is a way to satisfy a number of goals, from building up positive relationships in a group, developing physical and mental awareness to handling specific acting or staging demands. For a game to work most effectively, it is essential that each player willingly cooperate, support and trust his/her fellow players.

Theatre games is a way of solving problems. The problem is how to play the game. Because of the unpredictable progress of any game, this is the problem each player is solving each instant he/she is playing the game. How, for example, did you first learn to play a game when you were a child? You learned by actually playing it. Did you ever really finish learning to play the game? No. Each time you played, you played differently, sharpening and learning to trust your abilities, learning to play more skillfully. That is true of any game, whether you played it as a child or play it as an adult. Learning the process of solving the problem of how to proceed is the pleasure we take from a game.

These, then, are the fundamentals of improvisation—of theatre games and any other kind of games, whether there are two, five or thirty players. It requires a group effort or agreement, which depends on **Cooperation**, **Support** and **Trust** among the players. Its course is unplanned and open-ended, depending on each players spontaneous contribution in order to progress. It has a problem that can only be solved through action.

Samuel Elkind Ph. D.

Courtesy of the William-Alan Landes Collection. From the Pathé Pictures, 1930 version of Philip Barry's play *HOLIDAY*. (Left to right) Robert Ames, Mary Astor and Edward Everett Horton.

Improvisation: Theater Games

You already know more about improvisation than you may think you know. If you have ever played a game, you have experienced improvisation in its original form. In the theater, when games are played for the purpose of exploring and solving acting problems, we call the method improvisation. The fundamentals of improvisation are the same as those of a game.

A game is a group effort. Without a sense of group purpose, the knowledge that we are all playing the same game, there can be no game. And the purpose or goal is simply to play the game, to see what will happen between the beginning and the conclusion of the activity. Reaching that goal requires each player's willingness to cooperate with, support, and trust his fellow players. A pitcher and a batter, for example, even though they are on opposing teams, cooperate by agreeing to play by the same rules. They support each other's efforts by playing by those rules. Thus the batter can trust the pitcher not to aim the ball at his head, and the pitcher can trust the batter to attempt to hit the ball rather than to catch it.

But a game also depends on individuality, each player's uniqueness, his personal style of playing. Each player's imagination and spontaneous reactions add to the game, keep it moving and changing quickly. The course and outcome of the game are unplanned and unpredictable, for no player can be entirely sure what any other player will do next. Thus each game reaches its conclusion in a way different from all previous games. Individual spontaneity is the element of surprise which holds our interests, whether we are players or observers.

Playing a game is a way of solving a problem. The problem is *how* to play the game. Because of the unpredictable progress of any game, this is the problem each player is solving each instant he is playing the game. How, for example, did you first learn to play a game when you were a child? You learned by actually playing it. Did you ever really finish learning to play the game? No; each time you played, you played differently, sharpening and learning to trust your abilities, learning to play more skillfully. That is true of any game, whether you played it as a child or play it as an adult. Learning, the process of solving the problem of how to proceed, is the pleasure we take from a game.

These, then, are the fundamentals of improvisation—of theater games and any other kind of games—whether there are two, five, or fifty players. It requires a group effort or agreement, which depends on cooperation, support, and trust among the players. Its course is unplanned and open-ended, depending on each player's individual spontaneity in order to progress. It has a problem that can only be solved through action.

1

Games

The following games are steps toward the more complex improvisational methods that you will encounter in the next section of this handbook, where you will begin to improvise as a way of exploring a script and solving the problems it poses for you as an actor. These games are a way of experiencing the techniques of improvisation in a familiar form and of setting yourself up physically and mentally for the unique demands that theater activities make of you.

It would be a good idea to spend at least a couple meetings, at the outset of your study of improvisation, concentrating primarily on these game experiences. They will help establish the group solidarity—the attitudes of coopera tion, support, and trust—necessary for successful improvisation (and for successful acting in general). Thereafter, it would be a good idea to play a couple games for warming up at the beginning of each meeting. Perhaps you will have just come from taking a math test, from a class discussion, from a job, from lunch, or from an argument. Playing a couple games will give you a chance to loosen up and change mental directions. Games will help develop your physical, intellectual, and emotional readiness to respond quickly and unselfconsciously to the unpredictable and rapidly changing situations which are a basic part of improvisation. And they will reinforce and continue to build cooperation, support, and trust among the members of the group.

There are five groups of games in this section. The first two are *physical* games and *mental* games, which are a good place to begin. You will probably get the feel of them quickly and go on to more complex games. However, you will probably want to return to them for warm-up exercises for later meetings The next two groups are *trust* games and *support* games. Notice that there is no similar group of games especially intended for fostering cooperation. Cooperation is a natural part of *any* game, even if you play only grudgingly. Trust and support, however, come about through your willingness to give yourself to the activity, to interact intimately with the other players. Trust games help loosen up that willingness, and support games put it to use and strengthen it. Finally, there is a group of *awareness* games. Awareness games are experiences that will help you develop control of your responses—that is, your ability to observe a situation carefully and, *simultaneously,* respond to it appropriately. Try not to miss the awareness games. In a sense, they are a bridge between the earlier games and improvisation used specifically as a theater method.

The games are useful for more than just warming up. After some experience with them, you will be able to use specific games for specific purposes. Your intuition will tell you when a trust game or support game might be helpful to the group's spirit. There might be times when you sense that a vigorous physical game will help dispel tension, or that an awareness game might be helpful to group members practicing a scene. Any time you feel that a game might be of help—at warm-up time, while improvising, or while practicing a scene—suggest it to the rest of the group.

Avoid getting into a rut by playing the same games every day or always playing the games in the same order. Each player will enjoy and respond to some games more than to others. Vary your activities to keep as much interest in them as possible and to maintain room for individual experimentation. Change leaders when you begin a new game. Do not come to rely on one person always being the leader of a particular game. For games which require small groups or teams of players, change team members from game to game. However, there is no reason to play a game no one likes. After becoming acquainted with the games and giving them a fair chance, the group may decide to eliminate some games from its repertoire.

Avoid dulling your reactions with fatigue. Rest between games if necessary. Learn your own pace. Especially in games requiring repetitive gestures, be careful of starting with a gesture you will not be able to sustain comfortably to the end of the game.

Avoid "playwriting," planning a game out before (or while) you play it. Planning, in this sense, is the opposite of improvisation. Allow the game to develop as it will—within the agreed rules, of course. Some games require a leader, usually selected from among the players. The leader's job, however, is to organize and guide the game, not to control it or determine how the game "ought" to turn out.

The desire to compete arises in most of us from time to time. In improvisation, competition is usually wasteful. There is no best style of improvising. There is no best style of playing a game. In a sense, competition is a way of planning your actions out beforehand, of deciding *not* to react spontaneously. Allow yourself to make mistakes. Remember that your object is to play the games, to experience them, rather than to demonstrate how they best can be performed. Especially at the beginning of your work with improvisation, have patience and understanding—for yourself as well as for your fellow players. Selfconsciousness is a feeling even the most seasoned actor must deal with often. No one should be compelled or shamed into playing any particular game. Above all, respect your fellow player's actions. Accept them as his unique contribution to the game. React to them positively by building your own actions upon them.

These games are suggestions. They will get you started toward using games as a means of exercising your natural ability to improvise. They do not have to be played in the forms you find them here. For, as with all improvisation, there is no right or wrong way to play. This book does not set the rules; your group sets the rules. After some experience playing these games, ways of extending and developing the games will probably occur to you. If it occurs to you that a particular piece of music, for example, might add a new dimension to a game, suggest it to the rest of the group. What you see, hear, and experience in your daily life will give you ideas for altering the games and even give you ideas for new games. When ideas for games or warm-up exercises occur to you, try them. Present them to the rest of the group and serve as leader for your contribution.

PHYSICAL GAMES

Wounded Tag. This is a variation of the ordinary childhood game of tag, in which one player attempts to tag any of the other plavers, who in turn attempt to avoid being tagged. In this form of the game, however, when you are tagged you must hold a hand to the spot on your body where you were tagged, as though you had been wounded there, whether the spot is on your head, shoulder, or even your foot. You may release your hold only when you have succeeded in tagging another player.

Ball Game. Toss a basketball randomly among a circle of players. Do this long enough for each player to get the feel of the ball. Then "substitute" an imaginary ball for the real one and continue tossing it. You might also do this with a softball, balloon, medicine ball, or bedpillow (or whatever else might occur to you).

A variation of this game is to have a leader change the imaginary object while it is being tossed among the players. The game might begin with an imaginary basketball. As the ball is flying across the circle, the leader might call out, "It's a balloon." You would then catch the object as though it were a balloon, responding with your whole body to the weight, shape, and texture of a balloon. The leader might then call, "It's a cannonball," upon which you would imagine that you were throwing a small, heavy ball of iron and would adapt your actions accordingly. The leader changes the object at whim, perhaps from a bag of feathers, to a marble, to a light bulb, to a length of pipe. Imagine how you would use your body differently to throw each of these objects and how, for instance, the way you would catch a marble would be different from the way you would catch a basketball.

Jump Rope. Players divide into groups of three. Using an imaginary rope, each group plays jump rope games recalled from childhood. These are the games in which you jump the rope in time with such rhymes as "One Potato, Two Potato," "One for the Money, Two for the Show," "Bread and Butter," and "Alphabet."

Green Light, Red Light. A player is chosen to be the traffic light. He stands at one end of the room, while the rest of the players gather at the opposite end. The game begins when the traffic light turns green. He does this by turning his back to the other players and repeating the phrase "green light" over and over. While he is repeating, "Green light, green light, green light . . . ," the others may move forward. But at any moment the light may change to red by saying, "Red light." The moving players must then stop immediately. For when the traffic light has called, "Red light," he turns quickly. Any player he sees who is still moving, even if the player is merely tottering to keep his balance, must return to the starting line and begin over. The process is repeated until a player succeeds in making a round trip, moving to the opposite end of the room and back to the starting line, starting and stopping at the whim of the traffic light.

Players can move safely only when the traffic light is saying, "Green light." But the traffic light may attempt to fool the others by beginning with words which *sound* like "green light." For example, he may turn away, say, "Green *apples,*" and quickly turn back again. Anyone caught moving must start over. (No fair saying, "Green light, green light, green *apples.*" You can only change to "red light.")

Writing in Space. Everyone clasps his hands in front of him, prayerlike. With your clasped hands, carve the alphabet (or your name, or a word the group has agreed upon) in the air, using vigorous strokes.

Atmospheres. At the direction of a leader, the players move through a variety of imagined settings, conditions, or substances. For instance, the leader may tell you that you are walking through a dense forest. Imagine the humid air, the odors of decaying leaves and wood. Thick undergrowth catches your feet. You must protect your face from wiry twigs and bend branches in order to pass. Perhaps you have to climb over fallen trees, moss-covered and slippery. The leader may tell you that it has begun to rain. You become drenched and cold, and it is difficult to see clearly. He may tell you that it is now winter, and there are two feet of snow on the forest floor. How would the obstacles you would encounter in a snowy forest be different from those of a summer forest?

The leader might change the setting to a desert, then to a pit of quicksand, then to the moon where gravity is one sixth that of earth. With each change, let your imagination put you in the environment. What do you see, feel, hear, smell? How does your body respond to the unique properties of each environment? The environment might be a rationally impossible one, but make it real in your imagination. You might be up to the tip of your nose in gelatin. If the leader were to tell you that you were submerged to the waist in cornflakes, can you imagine how they would feel against your legs, how you would have to lift your feet to move through them, how your body would respond to their resistance, the sound they would make as you move? For variety, the leader might tell you that you are also a particular sort of character—a wounded soldier in a driving rain or a happy child in an enormous bowl of blueberries, for examples.

Simon Says. A leader faces the rest of the group. He gives a series of commands, each of which must or must not be carried out, depending on how the particular command is phrased. A command preceded by the phrase "Simon says" *must* be carried out. If, for example, the leader says, "Simon says, 'Touch your nose,'" you must touch your nose. But a command not preceded by "Simon says" must *not* be carried out. If the leader says simply, "Touch your nose," and you touch your nose (or even begin to touch your nose), you are eliminated from the game. The leader may attempt to entrap you by giving commands very rapidly, or by using a phrase which sounds like "Simon says." For instance, if he says, "Syrup says, 'Stamp your foot,'" and you begin to stamp your foot before realizing what was really said, you are eliminated.

Group Mirror. Players position themselves around the perimeter of the room. A leader stands in the center. The leader performs various movements, which the players imitate. The object is not to *follow* the leader, but for each player to move *with* the leader, as a reflection in a mirror. The leader's movements should have continuity, flowing gracefully and slowly, ballet-like. His movements should be large and clear, beginning with arm movements, followed by head movements, then movements of the entire body. Continue until the entire group is moving easily with the leader. You might find it helpful to perform the movements to a background of slow music.

Mirror for Pairs. The group divides into pairs. In other respects, this game is similar to a group mirror (above). One player of each pair is the leader; the other player imitates the leader's actions. The actions performed in a mirror for only two players can generally be more specific and intricate than in a group mirror, because the players can be physically closer. For examples, the leader might go through the motions of painting a picture on an easel, shaving his face, or making a cake batter. Ideally, an observer should not be able to tell who is the leader and who is the imitator. In fact, players may be working so well together that they exchange roles, from leader to follower, several times during the game, scarcely realizing they have done so.

Music can be a valuable part of a two-player mirror. For example, a Bach fugue or a two-part Bach invention may be used as the stimulus for a mirror game for hands. In such a game, one of the leader's hands might move with one theme, while the other moves to the counterpoint. Electronic or jazz recordings might similarly be used to create interesting movement patterns.

Things in Space. This is a game for players in pairs. One player imagines an object and proceeds to use or work with it. His partner then takes the object, and creates a different object of it. The first player takes the new object and transforms it into yet a third object, and so on. For example, a player might create a baton, imagining himself actually to be holding a baton in his hand. He conducts an imaginary orchestra with it. When the second player realizes that the object is a baton, he steps in and takes over conducting the orchestra. As he conducts, he lets his movements become broad and free. He lets his imagination work on the patterns he is making in the air. As the patterns inevitably alter and change, they might begin to resemble those of a fencing match. The player simply lets his movements develop along that new path, until they really have become those of someone engaged in a fencing match. (Notice, though, that you must try not to think your movements out. Just let them go and see what will evolve from them. It is something like discovering faces in clouds.) Thus, the baton has evolved into a saber. When this becomes obvious to the player's partner, the partner steps in and takes over the fencing match, and the cycle begins again. At times, a player might take an object from his partner but not be able to develop anything from it. If you sense that your partner is at an impasse, take the object back and develop it into something else. He can then take over the new object.

Word Journey and **Action Trip.** These two games are similar, and both are quite simple. But you may have to play them several times to get the knack of them. Try Word Journey first if you are unfamiliar with the games. You will probably catch on to it more quickly than to Action Trip. Both games are played in a circle of about six players. For Word Journey you might want to sit on the floor in a close circle. For Action Trip you will need to stand in a larger circle for greater freedom of movement.

Word Journey. A player begins the game by repeating a word over and over. (The first time you play you might start with the word "mambo." When you have gotten the feeling of the game, you will have an idea of what sorts of words will work best.) The rest of the players take up the chant. Use your natural voice; avoid droning. Continue chanting the word, all the players in unison. Let yourself get into the rhythm of the chant. As the chant goes on, you will find that the original word has begun to alter, though the players are still repeating in unison. Do not try to maintain the original word. Do not even try to keep the word sensible. It will probably become a nonsense sound. At the same time, do not *purposely* alter the sound of the word. Just continue the chant, letting the sounds emerge and develop as they will. Your object is simply to remain in unison and see what will become of the original word.

Action Trip. The basic pattern of this game is the same as that of Word Journey. Action Trip, however, is a game of actions. Your object is to remain in unison and see what will happen to an action as it is repeated over and over. A player initiates an action, such as rotating an arm or swaying his body. The rest of the players take up the action, and all continue it in unison. As the action continues, it will slowly begin to change and by subtle stages become a different action, though it is still performed in unison by all the players. Let this occur several times, always letting the actions emerge as they will. No player purposely changes an action. If the group is moving together well, you might continue until no further action develops. There may be times when no action develops from the initial one. In that case, let the game end, without feeling discouraged, and try it again at the next meeting.

When you have gotten the knack of these games, you might try them together. The leader initiates an action and adds a verbal sound. Let both the action and the sound change and develop as they will.

What I Was Doing. Players move freely about the room, each performing a variety of purposeless activities. For example, you might skip, spin, leap, turn your arms like a windmill—whatever occurs to you at the moment. Let yourself move freely and openly. At an unplanned moment, a leader calls, "Freeze!" You must stop in whatever position you find yourself at that instant, no matter how awkward or ordinary the position. Everyone must then invent a reason for being in his particular position. Forget the purposeless activity by which you had gotten into the position you are in. Concentrate on the position itself. Notice the arrangement of your hands, arms, legs, the direction of your face, the shape of your spine, etc. What might you have been doing in order to get into such a position on purpose? Picking a flower? Flying a kite? Helping a clumsy person climb out of a tub of ill-smelling chemicals? Your actual position and your imagined reason for it must be consistent. For instance, if you are standing on your toes and have one hand behind your neck, it will be difficult to convince anyone that you are picking a flower.

A couple variations of this game require the group to divide in half, into players and observers. The players begin the game, playing as described above, freezing at a leader's command. In one variation, the observers then invent a tableau, a story which includes and explains *all* the players' frozen positions. Another variation begins similarly. But, rather than creating a comprehensive story connecting the players' positions, the observers simply invent a reason for each player's position. (Remember that the imagined reason must be believable.) As a reason is assigned to his position, each player thaws out. He comes to life improvising the action which had been imagined for him. As the players improvise their individual actions, however, they are also aiming toward developing a kind of living tableau or loosely connected story, toward developing interconnections among each other's actions. For example, there are obvious possibilities for interaction between someone trying to loft a kite and someone who is picking flowers close by. But remember: you cannot plan the situation beforehand; you cannot *force* relationships to develop. Relax, let the tableau simply emerge and the relationships develop naturally as everyone follows his imagination.

MENTAL GAMES

Hot Potato. Players form a circle. (Depending on the size of the group, you might want to form two or three circles.) An object is passed from player to player around the circle. It might be a soft hat, for example—something that will not be damaged if dropped. This object is the "hot potato"; each player wants to get it out of his hands as quickly as possible by passing it to the next player. At an unplanned moment, the leader points to whoever has the hot potato at that moment and calls out a letter of the alphabet. Suppose the leader calls, "C!" The player with the hot potato passes it on as usual. But he must then say four words which begin with C before the hot potato completes another circuit. If the hot potato returns to him before he can complete four words, he exchanges places with the leader, and the game begins again. If it turns out that completing four words is too easy, try five, or yet six words. You want the game to be challenging but not impossible.

Playing the Letter. Players form a circle (or several circles, depending on the size of the group). A player is chosen to stand in the center. Any player on the circle's perimeter may call out a letter of the alphabet. The player in the center then performs actions which begin with that letter. If several players call out letters, the player in the center accepts the one he heard first. If someone calls, "*S*," the player in the center might begin to skip. The other players try to guess the word being performed, calling out their guesses. When someone calls "Skip," the player in the center immediately begins a new action. He might slip, slump, or turn somersaults; and the others again attempt to guess the word he is acting out. This goes on until the performer cannot change quickly from one action to a new one, when words beginning with *s* no longer come spontaneously to mind. Another player is then chosen to perform in the center.

Picnic. Players sit in a circle. A player begins the game by completing the phrase, "I'm going on a picnic, and I'm going to take . . . ." The second player repeats the first player's sentence and adds to it a second item. For example, the first player might say, "I'm going on a picnic, and I'm going to take an egg." The second player could then say, "I'm going on a picnic, and I'm going to take an egg and some salt." The third player might add a toothpick, and the fourth player might say, "I'm going on a picnic, and I'm going to take an egg, some salt, a toothpick, and mosquito repellent," . . . and so on around the circle, each player repeating, in order, all that has come before and adding one more item. You might want to adjust the number of players in the circle so the game can go around at least twice before the list of items becomes impossibly long. The group might decide on a "penalty" for players who do not repeat the list correctly. A player who leaves out an item or mixes the order of the list might be required to stand in the center and act out the list as it is being recited.

Rhyming. Players are seated in a circle. The object of this game is for the group to create a story or an extemporaneous oral essay, speaking in rhymed couplets, each player adding a line in his turn. Remember that this is a speaking game, not a literary exercise. Your rhymes need not be perfect. Though your meter need not be strict, it should be fairly constant. Try to speak naturally, avoiding twisting a sentence in order to make a rhyme. The first player's line establishes the topic, but the opening topic may alter greatly as the game develops. A player may create a line which is a complete sentence, or he may leave his sentence incomplete, requiring the next player to complete it.

Find the Leader. This is another form of the mirror games described earlier (page 6)—but with an added challenge. Players form a circle. One player is chosen to leave the room. When he has gone, the rest of the players choose a leader. The leader begins performing an action—such as patting the floor with his palms or rubbing his stomach—which the rest of the players in the circle mirror. The absent player is then called back into the room and stands within the circle. The action of the circle proceeds as it would in any mirror game. The leader begins to alter his action, by subtle stages developing it into a new action, which in turn changes into yet another, and so on. The imitators continue to mirror the changing actions. As the actions go on around him, the player in the center is allowed three chances to guess who the leader is. (But do not make it too easy for him. The imitators should avoid focusing their gazes on the leader. Nor should the leader make abrupt changes which will be difficult to mirror. Remember: the point is to perform actions *with* the leader, not after the leader.) If unable to identify the leader in three guesses, the player leaves the room again, and a new leader is chosen for him to identify. When he succeeds in guessing who the leader is, the player rejoins the circle. The leader then leaves the room, a new leader is chosen, and the game begins again. For variety, you might try adding sounds to the actions. You might also want to vary the number of guesses allowed, depending on the size of the group.

Simultaneous Conversation (for pairs). Do not be surprised if this game occasionally erupts with laughing confusion. Partners sit facing each other and agree on a topic of conversation. (It might be a good idea to agree also on a beginning signal. Each player might nod when ready, for instance. The second nod would be the signal.) Then the "conversation" begins. But it is not the same as an ordinary conversation. In this one, both parties begin—and continue until the end—to speak *simultaneously.* Actually, each is improvising a monologue explaining, describing, or simply expounding on the agreed topic. But at the same time, each should also attempt to give the appearance of actually conversing with the other. Speak *to* your partner, just as you would if you were really having a conversation with him and had his undivided attention. Look into his eyes and at his face as you normally would. And he, of course, is speaking to you in the same manner. Each player's aim is to stick to his own objective, to pursue his own monologue and not lose his thread of thought or pick up his partner's. However, you must not simply close your ears to your partner's voice. That would be as pointless as talking to a television. When your conversation is finished, each player summarizes what he has heard. Some amusement may result from comparing what was heard to what was actually said.

A variation of this game would be to have a simultaneous argument. Players would choose a topic upon which they could develop contradictory monologues—"for" and "against," as in a debate. Remember that part of the game is in creating the impression that each player is really arguing with the other. When finished, the players summarize what they have heard.

Two-way Conversation (for three). This game might sound complicated, but it is actually much simpler in practice. It is similar to the Simultaneous Conversation above. However, in the Two-way Conversation, the players who are talking simultaneously do not speak to each other; they both speak to a third player, who in turn attempts to respond to each of them.

Three players sit in chairs in front of the rest of the group. (Let us call the players Alice, Bill, and Cathy—A, B, and C.) Bill faces the group. Alice and Cathy face Bill, one on each side of him. The three decide on a topic of conversation. Then, Alice and Cathy, *both speaking at once,* begin asking Bill questions based on the chosen topic. You might think of the situation as taking place at a crowded party. Alice and Cathy are both insistently trying to get acquainted with Bill. But neither knows that the other is talking to him. Each talks to him as though the other were not present, as though she alone has Bill's attention. She repeats each question over and over until Bill responds to it. And Bill (a gentleman) politely attempts to cope with both questioners at once, answering all their questions, in effect developing a separate sensible conversation with each. The aim of each player is to keep from confusing the two conversations. When the game has gone on for awhile, on signal from a leader, a new player takes Alice's place, Alice moves to Bill's place, Bill to Cathy's, and Cathy returns to the group. The players may then continue with the same topic or decide on a new one.

A variation of the game would be for Alice and Cathy each to discuss a different topic with Bill. Alice, for instance, might begin a conversation about dogs, while Cathy asks questions about auto racing.

TRUST GAMES

Blind Walk. The group divides into pairs. One member of each pair is the blindman; his partner is his guide. The blindman lies on the floor, shuts his eyes, and relaxes. He keeps his eyes closed through this entire experience. The guide encourages and tests his partner's relaxation by gently lifting and lowering each of his partner's arms and each of his partner's legs. When the guide senses that the blindman is relaxed, he gently urges his partner to rise by lightly taking his hand or perhaps by lifting only a couple finger tips. When the blindman is standing, the guide lightly takes the blindman's arm, and the two of them start off for a walk. The blindman remains relaxed, trusting his guide to make certain he does not bump into objects or other players. The guide communicates with the blindman only through touch and gentle pressure. If conditions allow, the players may leave the room, even go outdoors. After about ten minutes, the guide directs the blindman back to their original position, and they exchange roles.

As the blindman, you may at first find yourself shuffling or stepping over-carefully because you feel anxious about stumbling or bumping into obstacles. Attempt to trust your well-being entirely to your guide. Relax, move easily. Experience your environment through your other senses. Notice the sounds, the odors, the movements of the air, the surface under your feet. The guide, too, should remain relaxed and avoid communicating anxiety to his partner. As the guide, try to avoid sharp, sudden stops and turns. Do not pull your partner along. At times, partners may adapt to each other so well that the guide need only occasionally touch or nudge the blindman to express his directions.

Sound Walk. This is a variation of the Blind Walk. The group divides into pairs, each pair consisting of a blindman and his guide. The blindman may choose to be blindfolded or to close his eyes. The guide moves away from his partner and begins to make a predetermined sound—jangling a key chain, tapping a pair of sticks together, or tapping a pencil against a drinking glass, for examples. The blindman moves toward the sound. The guide changes position frequently, always leading the blindman away from obstacles. If it appears that the blindman will not be able to avoid an obstacle, the guide may stop the sound and begin it again from another direction. If the sound stops, the blindman stops. When the game has gone on for a predetermined length of time, blindman and guide exchange roles. You might start by playing for a five minute period. The group can then adjust the length of the period to suit its needs. To avoid confusion, since several pairs will be playing at the same time, each pair of players should use a different sound for communicating. When you are the blindman, relax and trust your guide to direct you away from obstacles. Attempt to focus your attention on the sound your guide is making, following it without pausing to consider its direction. With a little practice, you will find that you can ignore other sounds in the room and that you become sensitive to very small changes in the direction of your guide's sound.

Falling Cradle. Players form a close circle. One player stands in the center. The player in the center folds his arms on his chest and falls in any direction. The others catch him and return him to his upright position. This is repeated until the player in the center can fall with complete confidence in the group's support. You will quickly learn to tell when this confidence is present by the player's manner of falling. However, it is the falling player, himself, who determines how long to stay in the center. Each player takes a turn in the center. Be sure the players forming the circle are close enough together and close enough to the center to catch the falling player easily.

Rushing the Circle. Players join hands, forming a large circle. A blindfolded player stands in the center. With his arms hanging relaxed at his sides, he rushes in any direction. When he reaches the perimeter of the circle, the other players gently restrain him. He then rushes toward another part of the circle, where he is again restrained. He repeats this until he feels he can rush the circle without anxiety, confident that the other players will support him. Each player takes a turn in the center. If possible, you might play this game outdoors.

Airport. Two rows of chairs are lined up to suggest the landing approach to an airport runway. One player is chosen to be the pilot, another to function as the control tower. The airport is engulfed by fog, and the pilot is unfamiliar with the airport. Obstacles such as books, clothing, and blackboard erasers are placed in the approach. The pilot is blindfolded. As he stands at the end of the approach, you might turn him slowly around several times to disorient him, or you might rearrange the obstacles after he has been blindfolded. The pilot then begins his approach. The control tower "talks" him through, around, and/or over obstacles. If the pilot touches an obstacle, his plane crashes. The game is over when the pilot crashes or lands successfully, and a new pilot and control tower take over.

Flying. The group divides into teams of at least seven players. A member of each team lies on the floor, relaxed, eyes closed. The other members of his team gather at his sides, lift him, still prone, carry him about the room for a few minutes, then gently lower him back to the floor. After resting, repeat the game with another member of the team as the flyer. When everyone has been lifted and carried, you might discuss your feelings and sensations with the rest of the group. Variations of this experience might be for the team to gently roll one of its members somersault fashion or to lift him prone and carefully toss him a couple inches in the air.

SUPPORT GAMES

Marching. The group arranges itself in marching formation—several rows of four abreast, for example. The group marches in formation about the room, following the commands of a leader. You need not know marching terminology; commands such as "Turn right," "Left," "In a circle," "Stop" will serve the purpose. After some practice in this manner, the group marches without the commands of a leader, relying on each individual's sense of the group's movements. Music might help unify the group during this experience. However, do not be too concerned if you cannot keep a perfect formation. Enjoy the group's flaws.

Mechanical Man. The players disperse randomly about the room. On signal from a leader, each player starts walking in a straight line, as though he were a wind-up doll. When he touches another player or an object, he pivots, making a ninety degree turn, and continues in a straight line until he encounters another obstacle, whereupon he again pivots and continues again in a straight line—and so on. You might add sounds to the movements, each mechanical person producing an individual noise when encountering an obstacle—"ping" or "beep beep," for examples.

Basic Machine. Any number may play. The group lines up against a wall. One player steps forward a few feet and begins performing an action in a mechanical, repetitive manner. He might raise and lower his arms stiffly at his sides, for example. One by one, in no predetermined order, the other players join him, each adding an action which in some way corresponds, or "interlocks," with the actions already being performed. The second player, for example, might bow from the waist in such a way that he always just avoids the first player's rising hand. But a third person might add an action in which he *does* touch one of the other players or even leans upon him for support. When you add your action, avoid doing so with the intention of making the machine develop in a symmetrical pattern. Instead, attempt to use your action to add variety to the machine. Adding movement at surprising places, in unexpected directions, and at various levels (such as lying down, squatting, leaning, standing) will help create interesting patterns. Your object is to create the impression of a fantastic machine, composed of individual parts which move in a complex rhythm, the purpose of which is a mystery. You might add a vocal sound with your action. You might produce a hiss at regular intervals, while another player might give a meaningless shout, and another make a cuckoo. Attempt to fit your sound into the rhythm of the rest of the machine.

When everyone has become part of the mechanism, let the machine go on functioning for a few minutes. A leader might then throw the switch which cuts the power, and the machine will glide to a halt. It might be interesting if the players were to hold their "off" position for a few moments, like a tableau, to feel the difference between being part of a still and part of a moving pattern.

If the group is large, three teams might be formed. When two of the teams have each developed an independent machine, the third team develops a machine which links the other two.

Variations of the Machine. The pattern for developing each of these variations is the same as for the basic machine above: one by one, each player adds an action, until everyone has become part of the mechanism. Unlike the basic machine, however, these machines have purposes—to "manufacture" a specific product, to perform a specific function, or to create a chosen impression. As you assemble a machine, be on the lookout for new ways to use your body to convey ideas, ways in which a single stance or simple movement or unexpected gesture can sum up a complex situation.

Product Machine. A player is chosen to be narrator. The narrator decides what the machine is going to produce. Then, as though he were narrating a TV commercial or a newsreel or conducting a tour of a factory, he begins to describe how the machine works. He describes each of the mechanical steps which lead to the finished product. He may be as whimsical or realistic as he wishes. As the narrator indicates for his imaginary audience each of the various mechanical parts and devices by which the machine functions, players step forward and become parts of the machine. A player adds an action which suggests the particular part the narrator is describing. For example, the narrator might begin by saying to his imaginary audience, "This machine produces little boxes of spaghetti. Here is the vat where the dough is made." A couple players might come forward and make a vat by kneeling and joining hands in a ring. Another player might become a mixer, and two others might become the mechanisms which dump the ingredients into the vat. "A big grabber comes down," the narrator goes on, "takes a lump of dough from the vat, and plops it on this conveyor belt." A player takes the part of the grabber, using his arms like a pincer. Several players, standing side by side, move their arms to suggest the conveyor belt. The narrator might go on to describe how the spaghetti is rolled into long strings, wound on a reel, dried, and so on, until a little box of spaghetti comes off the end of the machine.

Service Machine. A service machine differs from a product machine only in that it is based on a real machine which anyone might have encountered—a washing machine, candy dispenser, vacuum cleaner, printing press, pipe organ, etc. As in the product machine game, a narrator describes the parts of the machine, and players come forward to represent the parts. Again, the narrator may be as whimsical or realistic as he likes. The machine need only perform its service—washing a load of clothes, dispensing a candy bar, vacuuming the floor, etc.—no matter how fantastically it may appear to do so.

Machine For All Occasions. An all occasions machine is built upon an idea or theme. Unlike the product and service machines, however, there is no narrator to direct the machine's development. Each player contributes an action which he feels helps to convey the idea or illustrate the theme. The theme is based on any ordinary social activity. Your object is to assemble a machine which imitates how people act in that particular situation. But since a machine can imitate people only in a limited, unthinking manner, an all occasions machine is a way of making good-natured fun of our ordinary activities. Some possible themes are "dating," "theater intermission," "cast party," "committee meeting," "New York City," "Hollywood," and "holiday shopping." The possibilities are countless.

Suppose someone were to suggest "New York City" as a theme. A player might begin a New York City machine by rushing back and forth to suggest a hurrying shopper. (Remember that you are part of a machine; your actions should have a stiff, repetitive quality and in some way be timed with other parts of the machine.) A second player might perform like an aggressive driver, clutching the steering wheel, peering over the dashboard. A third player might act as though he were also a driver and collide with the first driver. He would have to arrange his movement so that the collision occurs over and over. Another player might raise his arm and call, "Taxi!" each time one of the drivers passes him. There might be a policeman who whistles, a businessman moaning that stocks have fallen, any number of pedestrians with crossing paths—and so on, each player adding an action which, to him, suggests New York City. The overall effect should be of mechanical human figures run by an unseen clockwork.

Monster. It would be a good idea to play at least one of the machine games (above) before trying this game. Creating a monster is much the same as developing a machine: one by one, in no special order, players come forward and add actions or movements which in some way fit with the actions already added by other players. The group's object in this game, however, is to create the impression of a sinister creature you could expect to cause some sort of unpleasantness for anyone who gets in its way. You do not plan beforehand how the monster will look when everyone has joined in. But you do have to keep in mind that a monster is living, rather than mechanical. While symmetry and balance generally are not important for making a machine, they are important for creating a monster. Like any real living creature, a monster should have right and left sides which are mirror images of each other. Suppose, for example, that a player begins the game by kneeling and proceeding to move his arm forward and back at shoulder level, suggesting some sort of antenna. A second player might then kneel beside the first, facing the same direction, and perform the same action with his left arm. Also, keep in mind the monster's personality. The action you add should help suggest the monster's menacingly sinister mood. A gesture might be claw-like, a movement of your foot might be lumberingly powerful, the way you move your shoulders might say, "I'm looking for a victim." The monster should be able to move—walking, creeping, or slithering—about the room. To do this, players will have to be more closely synchronized than in a machine game. To create the impression of a long body with many legs, for example, ten players might hold each other about the waists, front to back, and step in unison. You might add another dimension to the game by deciding to create a monster which lives in a cave, a swamp, or on a mountainside. A swamp-dweller, for example, might be long and slender and move by undulating or making slithery paddling movements. A mountain-dweller would be more suited for scrambling up steep slopes and moving or leaping among rocks.

Slow-motion. Players perform various activities in slow-motion, at a pace like that of a movie shown at, say, half speed. Movements and gestures should be large, flowing, almost overemphasized. The object is for everyone to sense and adapt to the group tempo. Slow-motion is also a good exercise for body control and for developing awareness of the small coordinated movements which compose a complex action.

Almost any physical activity can be used as the basis of a slow-motion game. The group might pantomime a baseball game or snowball fight. Music, such as works by Eric Satie, might be used as a background for establishing a mood for such activities. More aggressive activities, such as sword fights or shipboard battles (Hollywood-style), may work well for releasing tension. In such activities, players can use a variety of hostile and evasive actions—lunging, dodging, swaying, falling—all in slow-motion and without actually making physical contact. Imaginary obstacles such as a wall, moat, or swamp can help make interesting mock battles. A slow-motion activity can also be improvised around a musical theme. For example, players might improvise a bank robbery or an old-fashioned melodrama (with villains, heroines, heroes, maybe even a faithful dog) which proceeds with the movement of Bach's Fugue in C Minor. The effect is Keystone Kops-like, with exaggerated movements and gestures conforming to the rhythm patterns of the music.

Fast-motion. In this game, the group performs activities similar to those of the slow-motion game above—pie fights or cops and robbers chases, for examples. However, all movements and gestures are performed *faster* than normal. It might be fun to use background music in this game too—the *William Tell* Overture or "Flight of the Bumblebee," for examples.

Tableau. A group of from eight to twelve players begins by milling energetically or moving in several directions like a crowd on a busy downtown street. A leader calls out a word, whereupon the players freeze, forming a tableau which in some way reflects or illustrates the word. For instance, the leader might call, "Homework!" You would then quickly assume a position which displays your reaction to, or visualization of, the idea of homework. Your position may or may not relate to another player's position. For example, one player might appear to be reading silently; another might appear to be reading aloud to yet another player, who in turn might appear to be puzzled or to be taking notes. The tableau is held for about five seconds. The leader then releases the group, and the group again moves about until another key word is called. You might repeat this process several times, responding to a new key word each time.

While you are displaying your individual reactions to the key word, you must also be aware of the group as a whole. The object is to form a tableau, an overall picture, composed of individual reactions. If someone were to come unsuspectingly into the room, he should be easily able to guess approximately what the key word had been. Try to use a wide variety of stage positions, levels (kneeling, lying down, stretching upward, etc.), and gestures. You should not be finicky about composing the picture, but attempt to supply enough individual variety for an interesting tableau to occur.

One-word Story. Players sit in a circle. The object of this game is for the group to invent a coherent story. A leader begins the story by speaking a single word. Each player, in order around the circle, adds *one word* to the developing story. You should improvise quickly, without mulling; much of the fun of the game is in the unexpected turns the story takes. At first, you might develop a simple description around a theme such as "baking a cake" or "selling a car." With some practice of this sort, the group will go on to more complex and open-ended storytelling.

Fatal Story. A leader stands in front of a group of from ten to fifteen players. The leader is a pitiless, easily bored king, whose sole object in life is to be continuously entertained. The players are his courtiers. The king points to one of the courtiers. This courtier begins telling a story or narrating an incident. He continues until the king indicates another courtier. The second courtier then takes up the story and continues it—the same story—until the king cues yet a third courtier. If a courtier falters or in some way breaks the story line, of course the king sentences him to die. (That is, the courtier must pantomime a novel death scene.) The rest of the courtiers, a bloodthirsty lot themselves, are quick to advise the king of their own displeasure with any storyteller. The last living storyteller must point out the moral of the story. If he cannot, or if his moral is unsatisfactory to the king or the rest of the group (who are now ghosts), he too must die. The king gets his just deserts because he has no courtiers left.

Uncle Glug. Ten players stand in front of the group. Another player is selected for the role of Uncle Glug. Uncle Glug is a born storyteller. If you were to ask him the time of day, he would probably tell you about the winter it got so cold that all the clocks froze solid and how, to this day, clocks are still three months slow. Uncle Glug is the narrator in this game. The other ten players are his imagination. Uncle Glug narrates a story, which the players act out as he is telling it. As well as taking the parts of the story's human characters, players may join the action as animals or as pieces of scenery such as trees, rocks, or even a snowdrift. A player may at times choose to speak for himself, either for emphasis or simply because it would seem more appropriate for a character (or even an object) to tell his (its) own story at a certain point. The telling of the story might oscillate between Uncle Glug's narration and the firsthand words of the actors.

At first, the players might improvise to the telling of such well known stories as "Red Riding Hood" or "The Three Bears." With practice at this sort of improvisation, the stories will become less rigid, more open-ended and unpredictable, developing as much by the player's actions as by Uncle Glug's narration. Remember that it is the improvisation which is an end in itself, rather than the performance of a planned scene. The purpose is to gain experience in supporting a group effort, whatever direction the effort may take.

Advertising Agency. Four to six players act as an advertising committee, a sort of idea group or "think tank." The rest of the group makes up, and gives to the committee, a name for an imaginary product. The committee is not told what the product is, how it looks or what its function is. The product's name might be Toptads, The Fermit, Formula Seven, or any name you might think of that gives no specific information about the product's appearance or use. The committee then proceeds to develop a design or a sales campaign for the product.

As a member of the committee, your object is to discuss the product in such a way that if someone were to come unexpectedly into the room, he would not be able to tell that the players actually know nothing about the product. Suppose, for instance, that the committee has been asked to design and market a product called Toptads. A player might begin the discussion by saying, "Since they are green, I think each Toptad should be shaped like a watermelon." The next player might continue, ". . . Yes, and be about an inch long." "That way," someone might add, "a person can carry a day's supply in his pocket." "That means about six Toptads per package," a fourth might remark, at which a fifth player might add, "And there should be a message on the package about how to use them in an emergency" . . . and so on. The committee might go on to discuss billboard advertisements for Toptads, radio and television commercials, or perhaps a way to interest elderly people in Toptads.

You might have the discussion go around the "table," each player speaking in turn. Or, after some practice, the committee might prefer to have an open discussion, players speaking in no special order. Always attempt to add to and develop the previous speaker's statement. Avoid negative statements. Each player's contribution is an asset to the design idea or sales campaign. It should be met with an attitude of "Yes, and . . ." rather than "No, but . . . ."

AWARENESS GAMES

During a good part of each of these games, only one of the two players will fully understand the situation. Therefore, only by the players' support for each other can the game continue and develop. Remember: support your partner. Respond to him so that he, in turn, can respond to you. Every response is a stimulus for a further response. If you sense that your partner is at a loss for what to do next, help him by further developing your own action, by adding something more for him to observe and respond to. Always be willing to change direction and to adapt to the needs of the moment.

Changes. Agree on which of you will initiate the game. Stand face to face within touching distance of each other, each in whatever posture occurs to him at the moment. One player might have his arms crossed on his chest, and the other player have one arm raised at his side, for example.

Suppose you are in your positions and ready to begin. You are standing as in the example above. The player who is to initiate the action is the one with his arm raised. His aim is to create an activity, a living situation from these, as yet, meaningless postures. So, he takes a moment to study them. As he observes, in a sense he is asking himself, "Why might we be in such positions; what might we be doing here together?" Perhaps what occurs to him is that he is a parent and his partner is a child, whom he is trying to persuade to go into the house and practice the piano. So, he begins to act out the situation. He might attempt to persuade his "child" with promises of rewards. Perhaps he takes his partner's arm as if to maneuver him to the house. The other player, of course, does not remain passive during all this. Though he might not yet understand what the action means, he attempts to participate. He attempts to respond to his partner and actively go along with the situation until catching on to his partner's idea.

When the first action has been established in that manner (actually, it might have taken only a few seconds), your aim becomes to transform it into a new one. For example, your chance might come when the first player grasps the other's arm. The second player might respond by flinching and exclaiming, "Ouch! That's the spot, Doc!" Thus, the original parent-child relationship has been abruptly changed to a doctor-patient one. This new situation might then develop for a few moments until one of you, with a single gesture, creates yet a third situation with an entirely different environment.

There is no predicting when the changes will occur. One action might last only a few seconds before it is transformed into a new one. Another might develop for awhile before one of you senses a good point at which to change it. In the course of a few minutes of playing, you might find yourself successively in a hospital, on a safari, on a bus, in a balloon, and wading a swamp. You might become a child, a tree, a chair, a dog, a nurse, and a rich grandfather. Some actions will develop in silence, others will be verbal. There should be no breaks. The actions should flow together, each continuing until a new one develops from it. Each player must accept whatever changes his partner initiates and find a way to participate. You must work together, even during bizarre and sometimes bewildering actions.

You Have It, I Want It. Imagine two acquaintances—let us call them Jill and Helen—involved in the following situation. Helen owns a ball-point pen. Jill covets that particular pen and would very much like to have it. In fact, Jill wants the pen so much, that she proceeds to try to persuade Helen to give it to her—not as a loan but as an outright gift. But Helen is just as intent on keeping her pen as Jill is on acquiring it. So, not only does Helen refuse Jill's every appeal, but at the same time tries to convince Jill of her unwillingness to part with the pen. And thus their conversation continues. Every appeal prompts a refusal. Each refusal spurs a further appeal.

That is the situation of the game You Have It, I Want It. One player takes a role corresponding to Jill's, and the other takes Helen's position. But there is a catch to the game. The object, which Helen has and Jill wants, is known only to Helen. At the beginning of the game, Helen creates the object in her imagination. (It should be a specific object, such as a pen, book, article of clothing, etc.) But she does not tell Jill what it is. Their "argument" then proceeds as in the illustration above, but with Jill acting *as though* she knows what the object really is. Throughout the game, both players refer to the object only as "it," even if Jill eventually catches on to the object's identity.

Your aim in this, as in any game, is to keep the situation moving and see what will become of it. In this instance, that means you must avoid such simple dead end responses as "Give it to me" and "No"; such conversation goes nowhere. For instance, in Helen's role, you might refuse Jill by telling her that you cannot give it to her because your mother gave it to you a long time ago. What might Jill say in return? That Helen's mother has probably forgotten about it? That such sentimentality should not stand in the way of friendship? Helen, of course, would then respond with another equally determined reason or excuse. Though the game has no definite end, you will probably want to continue at least until both of you (especially Jill, who starts in the more uncertain position) are well into your roles and your responses come naturally. Ideally, an uninformed observer would be unable to tell that only one of you knows exactly what "it" is, and that "it" is purely imaginary, besides.

Who Am I? Decide which player will lead in developing the action of the game. The other player then leaves the room, closes the door, and waits to be summoned. Suppose you are the lead player. It is your task, after your partner has gone, to invent a premise, the basic situation which you and your partner will play out. That is, you decide on the role you will play for the rest of the game, on the role your partner is to play, and on what the relationship between the two of you will be. For example, you might decide that you are going to be a possessive mother, and that your partner is to be your son who is about to leave to visit his fiancee. (You do not want to be too specific about details at this time. You will improvise the details as the game goes along.) When you have thus decided what the basic situation is to be, you open the door behind which your partner is waiting. That is when the game actually begins.

From the moment you open the door, you are in your role. You *are,* in both mental attitude and physical manner, the kind of character you chose to portray. And you must act toward your partner as though he actually is the character you chose for him to play. You (to continue with the example above) are a mother who is jealous of your son's attention. And, this is your son at the door. You know that he is about to leave to visit his fiancee. From those few facts, you must begin to develop the situation. How, for instance, might you show your feelings toward your son? How would you feel about his fiancee? About the idea of his leaving to see her (of all people!)? Upon opening the door, you would have to improvise an appropriate greeting and a way of causing your son to enter the room. (Remember that your partner would not yet be aware of what the situation is all about. So, you must take the lead and get the scene moving.) You might say something like, "I'm so glad you had time to see me before you leave!" In an almost pleading tone you might add, "Won't you come in for a few moments, Dear?" Would you next attempt to dissuade him from leaving? Attempt to persuade him to break his engagement? Demand, cajole, play on his feelings? And so on. . . .

What would the other player be doing during all this? Suppose you are he. When the door opens, you would have no idea what situation to expect. You would not know whom your partner is portraying, whom you are supposed to be, or why you are here. Your object, though, would be to find out. To do that, you could not remain passive. You must play along, helping to carry the action onward by attempting to respond appropriately to your partner's actions—just as though you really were fully aware of the situation. All the while, you would also be picking up clues. In the example in the paragraph above, your partner's very first words would tell you that you are planning to go somewhere. And when she calls you "Dear," you would learn something of your relationship to her. But would that suggest that you are her son, brother, boyfriend, or husband? The tone of her voice, the way she moves, holds her hands, smiles or frowns would all give you more information about your relationship to her and the reason for your meeting. In her words might be clues which would tell you that the setting is your home rather than an office. Bit by bit, you become aware of your and your partner's identities and of what is happening between you. But remember: throughout the game, no matter how little or much you know about the situation, you are always a participant, always attempting to adapt your responses to your partner's actions.

There is no definite ending point to this game. It should continue at least until the second player has figured out his particular role in the situation and thereby becomes an equal participant in the scene. You might want to let the scene go on for awhile longer, just to see what might develop. Other examples of Who Am I? situations might be between a receptionist and a salesman, a rabbi and a troubled member of the congregation, an interviewer and a job applicant. Doubtless, your daily experiences will give you many ideas for interesting situations. You might also try the game with three players, two of them knowing the situation, the third in the Who am I? role.

2

Improvising with the Scene

In this section of the handbook, you will be improvising to explore specific scripts and to test various possible solutions to the problems they pose to you as an actor. Notice that word, "explore." An explorer sets out into an unfamiliar environment to discover what there is to be discovered there. Ultimately, his discoveries add up to greater knowledge and understanding of a formerly unclear region. In improvisation, your environment is a play or an individual scene—the hearts of its characters, its plot and setting, and the way those three elements work together as dramatic action. By exploring that environment with improvisation, you might, for instance, discover motivations for a character's behavior that are not apparent in the script. You might become aware of the playwright's purpose for having a character enter the action at a precise moment or the way the setting influences a particular action. Improvising with a scene gives you a chance to focus on such problems of characterization and plot development one at a time and to discover, through your own creative actions, the acting techniques that most effectively solve them.

There are scripts for eight scenes in this section. Following each script are brief comments on some of the problems it poses and descriptions of several improvisational situations you can use for attacking those problems. Generally, you will probably find that the best way to approach each script and its improvisations is to read the script, then work with the improvisations, then return to the script and perform the scene. After some experience, however, you can alter that order to suit your needs. For instance, at times you might want to use improvisations at certain points *during* your work with the script. Or you might want to adapt an improvisation that you had used to solve a similar problem in another scene. (You will find it helpful to read, when circumstances allow, the entire play from which the scene you are working on has been excerpted.)

Were there one basic rule to be adhered to at all times, it would be this: *an improvised action must happen in a definite place.* It should always be clear to a viewer that the action is occurring in a specific place; a viewer must be able to recognize that place at once. Before an improvised scene can really get under way, you must establish, either through physical action (stage business) or dialogue, that you are in a particular place, doing something other than just talking. By defining the site of the action, you have begun to establish the other two key factors of a successful improvisation: the *characters*—who they are, and what their relationship to each other is; and the *action*—what is happening, and why it is happening. Those three factors—place, character, and action—should be established before you let any sort of conflict develop. For, scenes that leap into conflict are usually quickly over, tending to defeat the purpose of most improvisations.

The suggested improvisations you encounter in the following pages are meant to be starters. Their point is to give you firsthand experience in using improvisation as a theater tool. Using them as a base from which to begin improvising, you will get the feel of the method and soon be coming up with your own ideas for improvisations. You are always encouraged to try out ideas when they occur to you. For instance, though many of the suggested improvisations give definite action sites, you are free to establish any setting you would like to explore or that you feel would be better suited to the problem you are working out. For, you must not take the improvisations suggested in this, or any, handbook to be the final word on improvisation. You and your fellow actors have the final word as to whether a particular improvisation is useful to you.

As you progress through the various scenes, experimenting and developing your improvisational skills, you will become your own best critic, distinguishing your more successful improvisations from your less successful ones and learning how to make the improvisations best work toward solving the problem. You will also discover why some of your improvisations do not work; you will thus be able to correct your approach and get going on the right track. With experience, you will be able to give form to your improvisations. Each will have a beginning, a middle, and an end, without padding or unnecessary detours; when the problem has been resolved, the improvisation will be over.

from

ANGEL STREET

ACT 1

Patrick Hamilton

Atmosphere is an important element of the play. (Vincent Price played Mr. Manningham in the first American production.) There is an air of despair and suppressed terror. It is an evening in 1880, the living room of an old house on Angel Street in a rather wretched district of London. The room is densely and darkly furnished in the Victorian manner. There is a fireplace down right, above which is a door leading to another room, and below which is a settee. Up right is a secretary desk. In the center of the room is a table with a lamp on it. There is a desk stage left with chairs above and below it. The front door is at the back. The room is lighted by the oil lamp, a coal fire, and a couple gas jets.

Angel Street is a thriller. As in most of our own TV detective dramas, the real motivation behind the action is not revealed until the very end, when the villain is finally exposed and apprehended. So, it would be a good idea to read the entire play.

Bella Manningham is deeply and blindly in love with her husband. Jack Manningham is about forty-five. He is tall, good looking, with a heavy moustache and beard, and dressed perhaps a little too well. Yet, in a mysterious way, his appearance seems suited to his dingy surroundings. His manner is smooth and authoritative. Bella is about thirty-four. Clearly, she was once a handsome woman. But now there is a sense of failing, of something haggard and frightened about her appearance. There are rings under her eyes.

Bella does not know that her husband is a criminal. Nor does Jack want her to know. He does not want to risk being exposed to the police. So, he has undertaken to make it impossible for Bella to suspect him. He is coldly and systematically attempting to drive his wife insane. He has been breaking down her self-confidence by confusing her and making it impossible for her to believe her own senses, by convincing her that she has done things that she cannot remember having done. That way, he can also make any clues to his criminal activities appear to others to be the results of Bella's irrational behavior. He treats Bella as a lying child. He terrorizes her with the possibility that she may have inherited her mother's insanity. Just before the present excerpt begins, Jack accused Bella of having secretly removed a picture from the wall. Humiliated and having no other defense, Bella snatched up a Bible and swore her innocence on it. Jack responded by grabbing the Bible away and declaring that only madness—like her mother's—could explain such sacrilege. When the excerpt opens, Jack is still holding the Bible.

MR. MANNINGHAM (*crosses Right. Pause*). The time has come to face facts, Bella. If this progresses you will not be much longer under *my* protection.

MRS. MANNINGHAM. Jack—I'm going to make a last appeal to you. I'm going to make a last appeal. I'm desperate, Jack. Can't you see that I'm desperate? If you can't, you must have a heart of stone.

MR. MANNINGHAM (*turns to her*). Go on. What do you wish to say?

MRS. MANNINGHAM. Jack, I may be going mad, like my poor mother—but if I am mad, you have got to treat me gently. Jack—before God—I never lied to you knowingly. If I have taken down that picture from its place I have not known it. *I have not known it.* If I took it down on those other occasions I did not know it either. Jack, if I steal your things—your rings—your keys—your pencils and your handkerchiefs, and you find them later at the bottom of my box, as indeed you do, then I do not know that I have done it— Jack, if I commit these fantastic, meaningless mischiefs—so meaningless—why should I take a picture down from its place? If I do all these things, then I am certainly going off my head, and must be treated kindly and gently so that I may get well. You must *bear* with me, Jack, *bear* with me—not storm and rage. God knows I'm trying, Jack, I'm trying! Oh, for God's sake believe me that I'm trying and be kind to me!

MR. MANNINGHAM. Bella, my dear—have you any idea where that picture is now?

MRS. MANNINGHAM. Yes, yes, I suppose it's behind the secretary.

MR. MANNINGHAM. Will you please go and see?

MRS. MANNINGHAM (*vaguely*). Yes—yes— (*She goes to upper end of secretary and produces it.*) Yes, it's here.

MR. MANNINGHAM (*reproachfully; as he crosses to the desk, places the Bible on it*). Then you did know where it was, Bella. (*Turns to her.*) You did know where it was.

MRS. MANNINGHAM (*as she starts toward him*). No! No! I only *supposed* it was! I only supposed it was because I found it there before! It was found there twice before. Don't you see? I *didn't* know—I didn't!

MR. MANNINGHAM. There is no sense in walking about the room with a picture in your hand, Bella. Go and put it back in its proper place.

MRS. MANNINGHAM (*pause, as she hangs the picture on the wall, then comes to the back of the chair right of table*). Oh, look at our tea. We were having our tea with muffins—

MR. MANNINGHAM. Now, Bella, I said a moment ago that we have got to face facts. And that is what we have got to do. I am not going to say anything at the moment, for my feelings are running too high. In fact, I am going out immediately, and I suggest that you go to your room and lie down for a little in the dark.

MRS. MANNINGHAM. No, no—not my room. For God's sake don't send me to my room!

MR. MANNINGHAM. There is no question of sending you to your room, Bella. You know perfectly well that you may do exactly as you please.

MRS. MANNINGHAM. I feel faint, Jack— (*He goes quickly to her and supports her.*) I feel faint—

MR. MANNINGHAM. Very well— (*Leading her to settee.*) Now, take things quietly and come and lie down, here. Where are your salts? (*Crosses to secretary, gets salts and returns to her.*) Here they are— (*Pause.*) Now, my dear, I am going to leave you in peace—

MRS. MANNINGHAM (*eyes closed, reclining*). Have you got to go? Must you go? Must you always leave me alone after these dreadful scenes?

MR. MANNINGHAM. Now, no argument, please. I had to go in any case after tea, and I'm merely leaving you a little earlier, that's all. (*Pause. Going into room up Right and returning with undercoat on.*) Now is there anything I can get for you?

MRS. MANNINGHAM. No, Jack dear, nothing. You go.

MR. MANNINGHAM. Very good— (*Goes toward his hat and overcoat which are on the chair above desk, and stops.*) Oh, by the way, I shall be passing the grocer and I might as well pay that bill of his and get it done with. Where is it, my dear? I gave it to you, didn't I?

MRS. MANNINGHAM. Yes, dear. It's on the secretary. (*Half rising.*) I'll—

MR. MANNINGHAM. No, dear—don't move—don't move. I can find it. (*At secretary and begins to rummage.*) I shall be glad to get the thing off my chest. Where is it, dear? Is it in one of these drawers?

MRS. MANNINGHAM. No—it's on top. I put it there this afternoon.

MR. MANNINGHAM. All right. We'll find it— We'll find it— Are you sure it's here, dear? There's nothing here except some writing paper.

MRS. MANNINGHAM (*half rising and speaking suspiciously*). Jack, I'm quite sure it *is* there. Will you look carefully?

MR. MANNINGHAM (*soothingly*). All right, dear. Don't worry. I'll find it. Lie down. It's of no importance, I'll find it— No, it's not here— It must be in one of the drawers—

MRS. MANNINGHAM (*she has rushed to the secretary*). It is not in one of the drawers! I put it here on top! You're not going to tell me *this* has gone, are you? (*Together.*)

MR. MANNINGHAM. My dear. Calm yourself. Calm yourself!

MRS. MANNINGHAM (*searching frantically.* I laid it out here myself! Where is it? (*Opening and shutting drawers.*) Where is it? Now you're going to say I've hidden this!

MR. MANNINGHAM (*moving away*). My God!— What new trick is this you're playing upon me?

MRS. MANNINGHAM. It was there this afternoon! I put it there! This is a plot! This is a filthy plot! You're all against me! It's a plot! (*She screams hysterically.*)

MR. MANNINGHAM (*coming to her and shaking her violently*). Will you control yourself! Will you control yourself!— Listen to me, madam, if you utter another sound I'll knock you down and take you to your room and lock you in darkness for a week. I have been too lenient with you, and I mean to alter my tactics.

MRS. MANNINGHAM (*sinks to her knees*). Oh, God help me! God help me!

MR. MANNINGHAM. May God help you, indeed. Now listen to me. I am going to leave you until ten o'clock. In that time you will recover that paper, and admit to me that you have lyingly and purposely concealed it—if not, you will take the consequences. You are going to see a doctor, madam, more than one doctor— (*Puts his hat on and throws his coat over his arm*) and they shall decide what this means. Now do you understand me?

MRS. MANNINGHAM. Oh, God—be patient with me. If I am mad, be patient with me.

MR. MANNINGHAM. I have been patient with you and controlled myself long enough. It is now for you to control yourself, or take the consequences. Think upon that, Bella. (*He starts to door.*)

MRS. MANNINGHAM. Jack—Jack—don't go—Jack—you're still going to take me to the theater, aren't you?[1]

---

1. Shortly before the beginning of the excerpt, Jack had promised to take Bella to the

MR. MANNINGHAM. What a question to ask me at such a time. No, madam, emphatically, I am not. You play fair by me, and I'll play fair by you. But if we are going to be enemies, you and I, you will not prosper, believe me. (MANNINGHAM *goes out.*)

IMPROVISATIONS

The relationship between the Manninghams is, on the surface, the relationship between a prosecutor and a defendant. But, *below* the surface, their relationship is that of persecutor and victim. That is a central problem of *Angel Street,* that each character has a different understanding of the situation and her or his role in it. Bella feels that she is truly a defendant; her motive is to convince Jack that she is not guilty of his charges against her. But she has not a chance; the prosecution is a frame-up. Jack is only playing the part of an objective prosecutor and only feigning moral indignation at Bella's refusal to admit her crimes. His ulterior motive, his secret goal, is to *persecute* her out of her mind, to destroy her.

Wife, Husband. This improvisation is a sort of sidewise approach to the problem of Jack's secret motive in the excerpt. We will call you Jack and Bella for now, but you may use your own names if you prefer; actually, you are just a husband-wife couple, whose situation has some similarities to that of the Manninghams in the excerpt.

Suppose that Jack would like to get rid of his wife, for he would inherit a fortune if she were to die. But he does not want to murder her and risk being caught. The player in the role of the husband must keep that motive in mind from now on. The player in the wife's role must keep in mind that she is *not* aware of her husband's hidden motive.

Suppose, then, that the two of you are members of a group of religious missionaries. Until a day or so ago, you had been on your way by plane to enlighten some benighted region of the world. But your plane had crashed, casting you, the only survivors, into an inhospitable wilderness. Having no provisions, you were forced to set out in search of aid. From that background, improvise an action along the following lines.

You struggle blindly through a swamp. You are dishevelled, worn out, and ill from exposure, thirst, and hunger. Imagine the heat and oppressive humidity. The place is infested with biting insects and, maybe, with snakes in the moldy trees and in the slimy water. How can you be sure that the animal calls, cracking branches, and unseen splashes are not the sounds of predators? In effect, you must imagine the setting clearly and bring it to life by

---

theater. But it is improbable that he had ever intended to fulfill that promise. More likely, he had held it out just to be able to snatch it away at this time and make Bella feel guilty.

reacting to it as though it were real. And Jack: remember that you would prefer that Bella not make it through, but you do not want to be the direct instrument of her death.

At last, you come upon a spring of fresh water. But Jack physically restrains Bella from drinking, knowing that she cannot survive much longer without water. Bella has no notion of what Jack is up to and can only think, in her own weakened state, that thirst has clouded his mind. What will you, as Bella, do? Try to reason with him? Plead? Trick him? Help him in what you believe is his distress?

Father, Daughter. This is an improvisation to help you get the feel of another dimension of the confused relationship between the Manninghams, for trying on the husband/father and wife/daughter aspects of their personalities. Imagine that Jack is an authoritarian father. He does not really care very much about his family, but he tolerates them when they do as he wants. Imagine that Bella is his rather shy and gentle daughter.

Improvise an action in which Bella approaches Jack, her father, and asks permission to use the family car to go to school this morning. She has good reason to ask; she has been ill, cannot yet tolerate the long walk to school, and has no friends who can help her. Jack's response, of course, is negative. Deep down, he considers the car his personal possession and does not want anyone else messing around with it. Besides, while Bella is trying to convince him to let her use the car, Jack is watering his collection of rare house plants and really does not want to be bothered with her.

Husband, Wife. One of the problems in the excerpt is that each character has something to hide. Jack does not want his ulterior motive exposed. Bella does not want to let go of herself completely and show how really terrified she is of insanity and of losing Jack. In those respects, this improvisation is parallel to the situation in the excerpt and will give you a chance to explore the problem of secrets from another angle.

Suppose the two of you have been married for many years but have been growing apart over the past while. Jack wants a divorce, but Bella is too dependant on your relationship to agree to one. Imagine, then, that the two of you live in an apartment in one of the uppermost stories of a very tall building. There is an open balcony off the living room. Improvise an action in which Jack, aware of Bella's terror of heights, attempts to persuade her to go out onto the balcony with him. As Jack, your real motive is to torment her into agreeing to a divorce. But you do not want to be open about it. Bella, in turn, does not want to show Jack how afraid she is of the balcony and actively tries to hide her fear. Both of you will have to get well into your roles for this sort of improvisation to work. As Bella, can you think of something of which you, personally, are afraid and relate it to your role? And, as Jack, you must really be cold, calculating, and convincing and find ways to use Bella's own fears against her. Notice, also, how particularly important it is in this situation to visualize the setting clearly.

Mr. Manningham, Mrs. Manningham. By the time *Angel Street* begins, the persecutor-victim relationship between the Manninghams is already well under way. But how might it have first begun? Establishing the reality of that unrecorded past event, actually experiencing it and making it truly part of Jack's and Bella's pasts, can help you to understand better their present thoughts and feelings.

Imagine that it is now sometime in the not-too-distant past. The two of you have been married and living in the house on Angel Street for only a couple weeks. You are planning your first dinner party, which is to be a rather large affair. Improvise a scene that takes place in your living room, during which the two of you are attempting to make the final arrangements about such things as the guest list, invitations, menu, time, decorations, and seating arrangement. This is just the sort of situation that you, as Mr. Manningham, have been waiting for in order to begin your campaign against your wife's mind. So, while appearing to be concerned about making sure the party will go well, you must actually be trying to plant the idea in your wife that she is forgetful, to shake her self-confidence by implying that she is too nervous, unreliable, or uncertain to handle such an important, complex affair. You must be subtle, for you do not want her to catch on to what you are up to. Remember: this is no spur-of-the-moment idea of yours; you have had it in mind since before you were married. In fact, the very reason you married Bella was to get her money and to have a mad wife as a cover for your criminal activities. In turn, as Bella Manningham, you must respond to your husband's implications and accusations by trying to reassure him that you *are* capable of carrying off this party.

Before beginning an improvisation such as this one, it is particularly important to take a close look at your character as he or she appears in the script, in the *present*. As an illustration, when you see two photographs of the same person, one taken in youth and the other in adulthood, it is usually obvious to you that it is the same person in each of the photos. In this improvisation, you are creating an effect similar to that of the two photos, the sense that the character in the improvisation is the same person who appears, years later, in the script. For example, judging from Bella's way of thinking, feeling, and reacting in the script, it would probably be unconvincing if she were to appear in the improvisation as a decisive, energetic, executive type. One of the points of this kind of improvisation is to get an idea of what it is in Bella's *nature* that has allowed her to become the nervous near-wreck that she is by the time of the excerpt. The present and the past must make sense of each other.

Bella, Jack. In portraying a conflict, such as the one between the Manninghams, your body movements and vocal quality are at least as important as the words you speak. In fact, memorizing the script is the easy part of acting; projecting the feeling and intention behind the words is your real business. You might say that voice and body are to conflict what lighting and props are to atmosphere. Here is a good exercise for concentrating on projecting, rather than just telling, the conflict between Bella and Jack.

Imagine that Bella has a message she wants to communicate to Jack. It is one that is very important to her. As Bella, you should not try to imagine any specific message. Just concentrate on your *need* to communicate it to Jack. Improvise, then, the two of you, a dance-like, mime-like series of actions. You may use no words, only nonverbal sounds, to express your feelings. Throughout the sequence, Bella must attempt to communicate her message to Jack. Jack, in turn, must continually respond negatively in some way to the message or Bella's attempts to communicate it.

Courtesy of MGM Pictures. Bella Manningham (Ingrid Bergman) and Mr. Manningham (Charles Boyer) from the 1944 film *GASLIGHT*, which was a studio renaming of the Patrick Hamilton play *ANGEL STREET*.

from

THE MISER

ACT 2, SCENE 6

Molière

The scene is set in mid-seventeenth-century Paris, the living room of Harpagon's house. There is a garden to the rear.

Harpagon is the miser to whom the title of the play refers. Possibly, he is the stingiest, most vain and self-seeking skinflint ever to appear on the stage. It is impossible to say which he loves more, himself or the moneybox he keeps buried in his garden; or which would cause him greater pain, a stomach ache or being asked to part with the smallest coin. Harpagon's miserliness is so excessive that he is ultimately more comical than despicable.

Now, in his sixties, Harpagon has decided to remarry. His object is Mariane, who is probably not yet in her twenties. To act as go-between in his courtship of Mariane, Harpagon has enlisted Frosine. Frosine is a woman who lives by her wits, by making herself useful to people, profiting as best she can from her talent for just such intrigues as Harpagon's courtship.

When the present scene opens, Harpagon is just returning from the garden, where he had gone to check his beloved moneybox. His opening aside refers to his having found the box secure. Frosine is waiting in the living room where he had left her.

HARPAGON (*aside*). Everything is going on right. (*Aloud.*) Well! what is it Frosine?

FROSINE. Gad, how well you are looking; you are the very picture of health!

HARPAGON. Who? I!

FROSINE. I never saw you with such a fresh and jolly complexion.

HARPAGON. Really?

FROSINE. How? You never in your life looked so young as you do now; I see people of five-and-twenty who look older than you.

HARPAGON. I am over sixty, nevertheless, Frosine.

FROSINE. Well! what does that signify, sixty years? that is nothing to speak of! It is the very flower of one's age, that is; and you are just entering the prime of manhood.

HARPAGON. That is true; but twenty years less would do me no harm, I think.

FROSINE. Are you jesting? You have no need of that, and you are made of the stuff to live a hundred.

HARPAGON. Do you think so?

FROSINE. Indeed I do. You show all the signs of it. Hold up your head a moment. Yes, it is there, well enough between your eyes, a sign of long life!

HARPAGON. Are you a judge of that sort of thing?

FROSINE. Undoubtedly I am. Show me your hand. Good heavens, what a line of life!

HARPAGON. How?

FROSINE. Do you not see how far this line goes?

HARPAGON. Well! what does it mean?

FROSINE. Upon my word, I said a hundred; but you shall pass six score.

HARPAGON. Is it possible?

FROSINE. They will have to kill you, I tell you; and you shall bury your children, and your children's children.

HARPAGON. So much the better! How is our affair getting on?

FROSINE. Need you ask? Does one ever see me meddle with anything that I do not bring to an issue? But for match-making, especially, I have a marvelous talent. There are not two people in the world whom I cannot manage, in a very short time, to couple together; and I believe that, if I took it into my head, I should marry the grand Turk to the republic of Venice. To be sure, there were no very great difficulties in this matter. As I am intimate with the ladies, I have spoken to each of them, of you; and I have told the mother of the design which you had upon Mariane, from seeing her pass in the street, and taking the fresh air at her window.

HARPAGON. Who answered . . . .

FROSINE. She has received your proposal with joy; and when I gave her to understand that you very much wished her daughter to be present this evening at the marriage contract, which was to be signed for yours,[1] she consented without difficulty, and has en-

1. Harpagon is forcing his daughter, Elise, to marry M. Anselme. The age difference between Anselme and Elise is similar to that between Harpagon and Mariane. Among the upper class, a formal engagement usually began with a contractual agreement between the two families, in many respects a business deal. The marriage contract

trusted her to me for the purpose.

HARPAGON. It is because I am obliged to offer a supper to M. Anselme; and I shall be glad that she share the treat.

FROSINE. You are right. She is to pay a visit after dinner to your daughter, whence she intends to take a turn in the fair, to come and sup here afterwards.

HARPAGON. Well! They shall go together in my coach, which I will lend them.

FROSINE. That will do very nicely.

HARPAGON. But, Frosine, have you spoken to the mother respecting the portion she can give her daughter? Have you told her that she must bestir herself a little; that she should make some effort; that she must even bleed herself a little for an occasion like that? For, after all, one does not marry a girl without her bringing something.

FROSINE. How something! She is a girl who brings you twelve thousand francs a year.

HARPAGON. Twelve thousand francs!

FROSINE. Yes. To begin with; she has been brought up and accustomed to strict economy in feeding. She is a girl used to live on salad, milk, cheese, and apples; and who, in consequence, will neither want a well-appointed table, nor exquisite broths, nor peeled barley, at every turn, nor other delicacies which would be necessary to any other woman; and let these things cost ever so little, they always mount to about three thousand francs a year at least. Besides this, she has no taste for anything but the utmost simplicity, and does not care for sumptuous dresses, or valuable jewels or magnificent furniture, to which other young ladies are so much given; and that comes to more than four thousand francs per annum. In addition, she has a terrible aversion to gambling, not a common thing in women of the present day; for I know one in our neighborhood who has lost more than twenty thousand francs this year at *trente-et-quarante.*[2] But let us only estimate it at a fourth of that. Five thousand francs a year at play, and four thousand in jewelry and dresses, that makes nine thousand; and a thousand crowns, say, for food: are there not your twelve thousand francs a year?

HARPAGON. Yes: that is not so bad; but this reckoning contains, after all, nothing real.

FROSINE. Pardon me. Is it not something real to bring you for a

---

usually specified the dowry that the bride would bring to the union. But Harpagon is hoping to negotiate a contract which will benefit his own moneybox.

2. A card game, which can be played only for gambling.

marriage portion great sobriety, the inheritance of a great love for simplicity of dress, and the acquisition of a great hatred for gambling?

HARPAGON. Surely it is a joke to wish to make up her dowry to me out of expenses to which she will not go. I am not going to give a receipt for what I do not receive; and I shall have to get something down on the nail.

FROSINE. Good gracious! you shall get enough; and they have spoken to me of a certain country where they have some property, whereof you will become the master.

HARPAGON. That remains to be seen. But, Frosine, there is something else still which makes me uneasy. The girl is young, as you can see; and young people ordinarily love only their equals, and seek only their society. I am afraid that a man of my age may not be to her taste, and that this might produce certain little troubles in my house, which would not at all suit me.

FROSINE. Ah! how little you know her! This is another peculiarity which I had to mention to you. She has a frightful aversion to young people, and cares for none except for old men.

HARPAGON. She?

FROSINE. Yes, she. I should like to have heard her speak upon that subject. She cannot at all bear the sight of a young man; but nothing gives her greater delight, she says, than to behold a handsome old man with a majestic beard. The oldest are the most charming to her; so I warn you beforehand not to make yourself look younger than you really are. She wishes one at least to be a sexagenarian; and it is not more than four months ago, that, on the point of being married, she flatly broke off the match, when it came out that her lover was but fifty-six years of age, and that he did not put spectacles on to sign the contract.

HARPAGON. Only for that?

FROSINE. Yes. She says fifty-six will not do for her; and that above all things she cares for noses that wear spectacles.

HARPAGON. You certainly tell me something new there.

FROSINE. She carries it farther than I could tell you. One may see some pictures and a few prints in her room; but what do you think they are? Portraits of Adonis, of Cephalus, of Paris, and of Apollo? Not at all. Beautiful likenesses of Saturn, of King Priam, of old Nestor, and of good father Anchises on his son's back.

HARPAGON. This is admirable. That is what I should never have thought, and I am very glad to hear that she is of that disposition. In fact, had I been a woman, I should never have cared for young men.

FROSINE. I should think so. A nice lot they are these young men, to care for them! pretty beauties, indeed, these fine sparks to be enamoured of! I should like to know what one can see in them!

HARPAGON. As for me, I cannot understand it at all. I do not know how there are women who like them so much.

FROSINE. They must be downright fools. Does it sound like common sense to think youth amiable? Are they men at all, these young fops, and can one love such animals?

HARPAGON. That is what I say every day; with their voices like chicken-hearted fellows, three small hairs in the beard twirled like a cat's whiskers; their tow-wigs,[3] their breeches quite hanging down, and their open breasts!

FROSINE. Indeed! they are well built compared with a person like you! That is what I call a man; there is something there to please the sight; and that is the way to be made and dressed to inspire love.

HARPAGON. Then you like my appearance?

FROSINE. Do I like your appearance! You are charming; your figure is worth painting. Turn around a little if you please. Nothing could be better. Let me see you walk. That is a well-built body, free and easy as it ought to be, and without a sign of illness.

HARPAGON. None to speak of, thank Heaven. Nothing but my cough, which worries me now and then.

FROSINE. That is nothing. It does not become you badly, seeing that you cough very gracefully.

HARPAGON. Just tell me: has Mariane not seen me yet? She has not taken any notice of me in going past?

FROSINE. No; but we have spoken a great deal of you. I have tried to paint your person to her, and I have not failed to vaunt your merits, and the advantage which it would be to her to have a husband like you.

HARPAGON. You have done well and I thank you for it.

FROSINE. I have, sir, a slight request to make of you. I have a law-suit which I am on the point of losing for want of a little money (HARPAGON *assumes a serious look.*); and you might easily enable me to gain this suit by doing me a little kindness. You would not believe how delighted she will be to see you. (HARPAGON *resumes his liveliness.*) How you will charm her, and how this old-fashioned ruff will take her fancy! But above all things, she will like your breeches fastened to your doublet with tags; that will make her mad for you; and a lover who wears tags will be most acceptable to her.

HARPAGON. Certainly, I am delighted to hear you say so.

---

3. Wigs made from flax fibers.

FROSINE. Really, sir, this law-suit is of the utmost consequence to me. (HARPAGON *resumes his serious air.*) If I lose it, I am ruined; and some little assistance would set my affairs in order . . . I should like you to have seen her delight at hearing me speak of you. (HARPAGON *resumes his liveliness.*) Joy shone in her eyes at the enumeration of your good qualities; and, in short, I have made her very anxious to have this match entirely concluded.

HARPAGON. You have pleased me very much, Frosine; and I confess that I am extremely obliged to you.

FROSINE. I pray you, sir, to give me the little assistance which I ask of you. (HARPAGON *resumes his serious air.*) It will put me on my legs again, and I shall be forever grateful to you.

HARPAGON. Goodby. I am going to finish my letters.

FROSINE. I assure you, sir, that you could never come to my relief in a greater need.

HARPAGON. I will give orders that my coach be ready to take you to the fair.

FROSINE. I would not trouble you, if I were not compelled to it from necessity.

HARPAGON. And I will take care that the supper shall be served early, so as not to make you ill.

FROSINE. Do not refuse me the service which I ask of you. You would not believe, sir, the pleasure which . . . .

HARPAGON. I must be gone. Some one is calling me. Till by-and-by.

FROSINE (*alone*). May ague seize you, and send you to the devil, you stingy cur! The rascal has resisted firmly all my attacks. But I must, for all that, not abandon the attempt; and I have got the other side, from whom, at any rate, I am certain to draw a good reward.

IMPROVISATIONS

The paradox of miserliness is that, even with a great stack of money, a miser has no wealth. Miserliness is more a state of mind and spirit than of finances. Besides being unable, by nature, to give anything to others, a miser is unable to give anything to himself. Perhaps that is why Harpagon so eagerly laps up Frosine's flattery: he is starved for self-respect.

Frosine, Harpagon. Notice how the action of this excerpt from *The Miser* progresses with wave-like peaks and troughs. Frosine builds Harpagon to a peak of enthusiastic narcissism; Harpagon slides back into a trough of self-doubt; Frosine builds him up again; and so on. There is the feeling of a game to the whole thing. So, here is an idea for an improvisation that is part drama and part game, paralleling the situation in the excerpt.

Imagine a men's section in a department store. Harpagon has come in to buy some new clothes. His vanity makes him want to appear stylish, but he is out of touch with current fashion; he is fussy about his appearance but rather gullible at the same time. Frosine is the salesperson he encounters. However, she knows at a glance that there is not a garment in the store that will come near to fitting this customer. But she is determined to sell him a garment anyway, so she can collect a commission from the store.

Here, then, is the game plan. You might call the game "I don't like it/Yes, but . . . ." Frosine presents Harpagon with a garment—a coat, say—that obviously does not fit him at all. Harpagon, of course, comments negatively on the fit of the coat. Frosine, then, must try to turn Harpagon's vanity against him, to convince him that the fault he finds with the coat is actually an attribute that makes the thing especially worth buying. To Harpagon's remark about the coat's poor fit, she might, for example, reply, "Yes, but that's all the *more* reason to buy it, for loose-fitting coats are the rage this season." That, naturally, is just what Harpagon likes to hear; so, at least for a moment, his negative attitude brightens, and he is pleased with his appearance in such a fashionable coat. But, being basically fussy and unpleasable, he must then find another fault with the coat. And, so, the process starts again. He might, for example, next say, "But I don't like this shade of green." To that, Frosine might reply, "Yes, but it goes so well with your handsome eyes—all the more reason to buy it." Thus the game continues, Harpagon accepting but then rejecting each of Frosine's sales pitches, Frosine responding to each of Harpagon's rejections with a new pitch.

All this is only the basic idea of the action. Each of you must help flesh it out and make a scene of it by fully taking on your role and behaving as though you really were the devious, opportunistic salesperson or the naive, fussy customer. Throughout the scene, attempt to find ways of using facial expressions to share with the audience your real feelings about the transactions taking place within the scene. The improvisation might end when Frosine has exhausted her arguments for the coat. Or you might go on to other garments. Either of you could easily change the direction of the scene by bringing a new element into it. For example, if the business with the coat were not working out well, one of you could have shifted the focus of the action to a pair of enormous trousers. In any case, you should try not to end the scene by leaving it hanging in mid air. Try to end definitely. For examples, Harpagon might stalk out, or Frosine might throw him out.

Harpagon, Frosine. This improvisation is a theater game in the same sense as the one just above. It is an exercise in the sense that it will help you focus your awareness on precisely what you are feeling each moment you are engaged in the action. That way, you will be able better to control your portrayal, the feelings, both overt and covert, that you want the audience to perceive via your vocal quality and actions. For this improvisation, you will be playing the characters as they were drawn by the playwright, transferring them by imagination to a new time and setting.

Suppose Harpagon is a member of a modern health club, which is owned and operated by Frosine. Imagine, then, that Harpagon is in the exercise room of the club. There are all sorts of muscle-building equipment and mechanical exercise devices. This is the first time he has used the exercise room, and his objective is to try out all the devices. It is Frosine's business, as an exercise therapist, to help Harpagon use the equipment. But, her feelings are not as simple as Harpagon's. She does not like Harpagon. Secretly, she would like to see him break his neck on the equipment. On the other hand, even though he has not paid his bill for several months, she needs all the business she can get in order to keep her club open. So, despite her real feelings, her objective is to make sure Harpagon does not hurt himself on the equipment.

From the motives described above, improvise a scene in which Frosine guides Harpagon from exercise to exercise. At the same time, however, you must verbalize your every action and the feelings and motives behind it. For example, if Harpagon were on an imaginary stationary bicycle, he might say, "I am riding this bicycle, and it is giving me a kink in the back." Frosine, then, might say, "I would love to see you hurt, but I am not going to let you ride this anymore, so I am taking you by the hand and helping you off." Either of you may then turn the action toward another device, verbalizing the action as you do so.

Harpagon, Frosine. In this exercise, rather than create an alternate situation for the two characters, you will improvise the situation of the script itself. Of course, you will have to have read the script and have a good idea of your character's particular objectives in the relationship and of how the action develops. For this particular exercise, the two of you will, first, have to agree on a floor plan (including doors and windows) for Harpagon's living room and furnish it. Makeshift props will do—whatever chairs, tables, etc., that are at hand. Then, improvise the scene, each in his or her character—but *blindfolded.* This is a good way to become familiar with the "space" of *The Miser,* for it forces you to focus on your movements within the set and on your partner's position. Naturally, you will bump into props from time to time. When you do, you must justify it; that is, attempt to create the impression that you have a purpose for contacting that particular prop. For instance, were Harpagon to bump into a desk, he might open a drawer to search for a missing jewel and, by his manner, create the impression that he is concerned about something but does not want Frosine to know what or why. Though not in the script, that is an action that would be perfectly in character for Harpagon.

from

THE MISER

ACT 4, SCENE 7

Molière

The setting is Harpagon's living room in mid-seventeenth-century Paris. Out of sight, to the rear, is a garden. (See page 34 for further background.)

Harpagon literally loves his money. His love is as huge as his vanity. His heart is a moneybag, filled full, with no room for anything or anyone else.

Just before this scene, Harpagon had had a frustrating argument with his son. The son had finally gotten fed up with Harpagon's self-centered tyranny and had graciously accepted the old miser's paternal curse. To a man such as Harpagon, that is treachery in its worst form. Was it for that reason that Harpagon had then gone into the garden—to seek solace from his beloved moneybox hidden there? For, when the present scene opens, Harpagon is in his garden. He discovers that his moneybox has been stolen.

HARPAGON (*aloud, shouting in the garden, rushing in without his hat*). Thieves! Murder! Stop the murderers! Justice! just Heaven! I am lost! I am killed; they have cut my throat; they have stolen my money. Who can it be? What has become of him? Where is he? Where does he hide himself? What shall I do to find him? Where to run? Where not to run? Is he not there? Who is it? Stop! (*To himself, pressing his own arm.*) Give me back my money, scoundrel. . . . Ah, it is myself! My senses are wandering, and I do not know where I am, who I am, and what I am doing. Alas! my poor money! my poor money! my dearest friend, they have deprived me of you; and as you are taken from me, I have lost my support, my consolation, my joy: everything is at an end for me, and I have nothing more to do in this world. Without you, life becomes impossible. It is all over; I am utterly exhausted; I am dying; I am dead; I am buried. Is there no one who will resuscitate me by giving me back my beloved money, or by telling me who has taken it?[1] Eh, what do you say? There is no one. Whoever he is who has done this, he must have carefully watched his hour; and he has just chosen the time when I was speaking to my wretch of a son. Let us go. I must inform the authorities, and have the whole of my household examined; female-servants, male-servants, son, daughter, and myself also. What an assembly! I do not look at anyone whom I do not suspect, and everyone seems to be my thief. Eh! what are they speaking of yonder? of him who has robbed me? What noise is that up there? Is it my thief who is there? For pity's sake, if you know any news of my thief, I implore you to tell me. Is he not hidden among you? They are all looking at me, and laughing in my face, You will see that they have, no doubt, a share in the robbery. Come quickly, magistrates, police-officers, provosts, judges, instruments of torture, gibbets, and executioners. I will have the whole world hanged; and if I do not recover my money, I will hang myself afterwards.

---

1. Harpagon begins addressing the audience.

IMPROVISATIONS

Harpagon is a ridiculous figure, accusing everyone in sight, even himself, of being the thief of his money. Yet, despite Harpagon's comically grotesque reaction to the theft, we cannot dismiss that his despair and confusion are real to him.

Harpagon. Here is an improvisation for focusing on your body as a vehicle for meaning. It is a means of exploring the ways your facial muscles, eyes, mouth, hands, fingers, torso, knees—all parts of your body—can be used to project Harpagon's confusion of fear, anger, sorrow, and suspicion.

Imagine that each side of your body has an independent will of its own. Your left side does not trust your right side. Your head is the judge or peace keeper. Improvise an action, without props, in which you are arranging objects on bookshelves or in a display case. You could imagine yourself as a junior clerk in a jewelry store or an apprentice librarian left alone in the rare collections room. Whatever conditions you decide on, you should be alone in the setting. What makes Harpagon more than just a comic figure is that his confusion is so human. He feels he must do *something* but does not know what or in which direction.

Imagine that you are the maitre d' of a restaurant. You are talking on the phone with your wife. She has an important errand to do but cannot leave the house, because you took her wallet and car keys by mistake when you left home for the restaurant. She is hysterical, and you do not want to hang up until you can straighten out the problem or at least until she has calmed down. Now, at the same time as all that is going on, your chef is trying to talk to you from the kitchen offstage. He urgently needs your advice about an intricate recipe. He has trouble understanding you because of the distance, and he cannot leave his stove. You must deal with both emergencies at once.

Imagine that you are alone in a junk yard. To anyone else, it would appear that there is absolutely nothing of value to be found here. But you are Harpagon, to whom there is no such thing as a valueless object, and who can never throw anything away. Improvise a scene, in pantomime, in which you pick through the junk yard, discovering such valuable imaginary things as stinking orange peels, dirty rags, rusty cans and nails, worn-out shoes, etc. You must identify each item you pick up by the way you handle, respond to, or otherwise use it. At the same time, you must invent a value for the item. That is, your actions must make clear that the item has great value and must be preserved so that it can be sold later.

Courtesy of the University of Santa Barbara Theatre Department (UCSB, campus photography). A scene from Molière's comic farce *THE MISER*.

from

TAKE A GIANT STEP

ACT 2, SCENE 1

Louis Peterson

The Scott family lives in an ordinary house on a quiet, tree-lined, middle-class street in a town in New England. It is a house that has been cared for with devotion, which gives a valid impression of the feelings among the people who live in it. This scene takes place inside the Scott home. The furnishings are not expensive or exceptional, but they are adequate, comfortable, and all in good shape. There is a staircase to the rear of the set.

The play is about the year of Spence Scott's transition from boyhood to manhood and the problems that Spence encounters during that year of impatience, the problems of an evolving human being in general, and those specifically of a middle-class black boy living in a white section of town. Spence is the younger son of Lem and May Scott. Their older son is away at college. Spence is high school age. He is an intelligent person, bright, curious, straight forward, who likes to think for himself. His interests and pastimes are typical of boys his age. And so are his dissatisfactions.

Spence is increasingly annoyed and impatient with what he feels are the arbitrary restrictions that the world places on him because of his age and his color. He feels hemmed in. He feels that he is ready to be a man, but that the world refuses to accept him as one. He feels that he has a natural right to be regarded as an individual person, but that the world around him refuses to respect that right.

When this scene opens, it is a little past ten in the evening. Spence has just come home much later than usual and found his father waiting up for him. Lem is angry. Lem had been concerned about Spence's safety and is the sort of person who grows angry as he worries. May Scott guesses from Spence's manner that he is in some sort of trouble. The voice of Grandma, May's semi-invalid mother, will be heard from upstairs later in the scene but can be cut. Grandma is a rebellious old lady with a quick, sharp wit, who is Spence's ally against all forms of oppression.

MAY. Are you in trouble, Spence?

SPENCE. I sure am.

MAY. What happened?

SPENCE. I—got kicked out of school.

LEM (*crosses to Left*). Well, I'll be good and damned.

MAY. Do you know what you did that was wrong?

LEM (*crossing to Right*). The little genius gets kicked out of school.

SPENCE. I don't think that I honestly did anything that was wrong.

LEM. That cinches it. He gets kicked out of school for doing nothing.

SPENCE. I didn't mean that, Pop. I didn't mean that I didn't do anything. I just felt that I was justified.

MAY. What happened, Spence?

SPENCE. Look, Mom—I don't want to go through all that again. I don't feel like it. (*Crosses to ottoman down stage of* MAY.) The teacher, Miss Crowley, that is, said something about Negroes. I was sitting there. I told her she was wrong. She got mad—I got mad. I walked out of her room and went into the Men's Room. I was mad so I smoked a cigar. (*Sits on ottoman.*) They caught me and brought me down to the principal. They threw me out of school for a week. That's all there was to it.

LEM (*moves to* SPENCE). What are you talking about—that's all there was to it? We got a genius on our hands, May. He knows more than the teacher. What do you think of that? (*Turning on* SPENCE.) Where did you get that cigar?

SPENCE. Out of your box.

LEM (*to* MAY). There you are!

MAY. In other words you stole cigars from your father?

SPENCE. I wouldn't exactly call it that.

LEM. Well, that's damn well what I'd call it. (*Crosses to above chair Right.*)

MAY. You and I will go back to school Monday, Spence, and you will apologize to Miss Crowley and be reinstated in school.

SPENCE. There's a week's vacation.

MAY. Then we will go up on the following Monday.

SPENCE. I don't think I can see my way clear to doing that, Mom.

MAY (*crosses sofa table for knitting*). There will be no more discussion about it, Spence. A week from Monday—and it's settled.

SPENCE. I'm not going up to school with you, Mom. I'm going to stay out for the week. I won't go back to school and apologize to anyone.

MAY. You want to disobey both your father and me?

SPENCE. I don't want to disobey either of you. I kind of felt that you'd be on my side.

LEM. You'll do what you're told. (*Comes down stage.*)

SPENCE. I suppose you can make me go up there with you—but I won't apologize to anyone.

LEM. Stop talking back to your mother.

SPENCE. I'm not talking back to her. I just want her to understand how I feel.

(MAY *is above* SPENCE.)

LEM (*crossing to* SPENCE). We don't care how you feel. Now, what do you think of that? You talk about what you'll do and what you won't. We do things we don't like to do every day of our lives. I hear those crumbs at the bank talking about niggers and making jokes about niggers every day—and I stay on—because I need the job—so that you can have the things that you need. And what do you do? You get your silly little behind kicked out of school. And now you're too proud to go back. (*Crosses up Right.*)

GRANDMA. Will you listen to him running his big mouth.

MAY (*crossing down*). Mama. We've given you boys everything that you could possibly want. You've never been deprived of anything, Spence. I don't need to tell you how hard we both work, and the fact that I'm in pain now doesn't seem to make any difference to you. I have arthritis in my wrist now, so badly that I can barely stand it, and it certainly doesn't help it any to hear you talk like this.

SPENCE. I'm sorry your wrist hurts, Mom.

MAY (*crosses Right*). You're not sorry at all. If you were, you'd do something about it. We've bent every effort to see that you were raised in a decent neighborhood and wouldn't have to live in slums because we always wanted the best for you. But now I'm not so sure we haven't made a terrible mistake—because you seem not to realize what you are—and you have no business talking back to white women, no matter what they say or what they do. If you were in the South you could be lynched for that and your father and I couldn't do anything about it. So from now on my advice to you is to try and remember your place.

SPENCE. You'll pardon me for saying so—but that's the biggest hunk of bull I've ever heard in my whole life.

LEM (*crossing down to him*). What's that you said?

SPENCE (*rises*). You both ought to be ashamed to talk to me that way.

LEM (*walks over and slaps him full across the face*). Now go upstairs and don't come down until you can apologize to both of us. Go on.

SPENCE (*crosses to foot of stairs, stops second step.* MAY *crosses down Right*). I'll go upstairs, Pop, because you're my father and I still have to do what you tell me. But I'm still ashamed of you and I want you both to know it. (*He is walking upstairs.*)

LEM (*crossing to foot of stairs*). That smart mouth of yours is going to get you into more trouble if you don't watch out. (SPENCE *has disappeared.* LEM *crosses down Right*). It's those damn books you've been reading—that's the trouble with you.

IMPROVISATIONS

Spence has one idea of what is good for him, his parents have another, and neither side is willing to retreat an inch. What makes the situation so difficult and confusing for all involved is that they really care about each other.

Spence, May, Lem, Classmates, Teacher. Though Spence's confrontation with his history teacher, Miss Crowley, occurred prior to the action of the play, from a couple descriptions of the event, it seems clear that Miss Crowley actually had made a naively disparaging remark to the effect that there is little record of black participation in the Civil War because the slaves had been too lazy to help themselves. Her remark had probably been merely ignorant, rather than intentionally cruel. The greatest part of Spence's rebuttal to the racial slur seems to have been a reaction to the childish snickers, whispers, and smirking glances of his white classmates. Based on those possibilities, improvise a scene that is a flashback to that time in Miss Crowley's history class. In effect, you are to make a reality of hearsay. However, there is one aspect that will be wholly new. That is, imagine that May and Lem are *classmates* of Spence. Spence, May, and Lem are the only blacks in the entire school. The attitudes of each toward blackness remain as depicted by the playwright in the present excerpt.

Another angle from which to explore the same ideas would be for Lem and May to keep their roles as Spence's parents. Improvise a scene based on the event above, but with Lem and May as visiting parents.

Lem, Spence. The relationship between Lem and Spence is a close one. Even in conflict, each would have an understanding, even if unspoken, of the other's style of thinking and feeling. That kind of mutual awareness is the reality surrounding *any* relationship and is what you want to project through your characterizations of Lem and Spence. This improvisation is a method for developing that sense of understanding. It is a form of improvisation that is especially useful when you have already begun to work with the script.

The actor who plays Spence in the excerpt takes the role of a father, and the actor who is Lem in the excerpt becomes the father's son. Devise, then, a situation in which the father discovers some unexpected object or objects around the house, in the garage, or some other appropriate place. It appears to him that the objects had been hidden there. He concludes that they are stolen. He suspects his son and his son's friends as the culprits. There results a confrontation between father and son. As the father, first you will have to invent the imaginary "stolen" goods (a TV set, a couple bicycles, some athletic equipment bearing the name of a local school for examples). Then, you will have to invent a believable reason for your suspicions (some kind of recent news story or some related past event, perhaps). But it might be a good idea not to tell your partner, at first, what items you have found. That will give him a chance to be surprised by the confrontation. For, as the son, you are not guilty; so, when confronted, you will have to invent an alibi for the presence of the object or objects.

May, Lem. Suppose the two of you, with Spence, who is only six, have just moved from a ghetto neighborhood into a new apartment in an all white neighborhood. Lem is not sure that the move was a wise one. He is uncomfortable in the new environment, because he is afraid that his background has not prepared him for dealing with the kinds of problems that might develop here. May, however, is determined to make a go of it; she is adamant in her belief that the move was both wise and necessary, that this is the only way that Spence can be properly brought up.

Imagine, now, that Spence has just been sent to his room as punishment for fighting with some white children, who, according to Spence, had taunted him because of his color. Improvise a scene in which the two of you are now unpacking your belongings. Your objectives are simply to reveal your feelings about the move. You have a couple possible courses. You might use a discussion of Spence's incident as the vehicle for expression. Or, on the other hand, you might simply go about your unpacking in silence, letting your physical actions and reactions reveal your thoughts and feelings about the situation and each other.

Cast. This is a suggestion for exploring ways of grouping yourselves at specific moments during the action, for developing effective *physical* pictures that will help make clear to the audience the changes in the *emotional* relationships among the three characters. In a sense, this is an extension of the support game "Tableau." You will have to have studied the excerpt rather closely. For, your object is to create a series of tableaux which tells the story of the excerpt. Your tableaux should make clear to the rest of the group what the excerpt is all about. However, you should try to avoid overdoing the story with too many tableaux. It might be a good idea to aim for as few tableaux as possible. The group's reaction will let you know if you have too few. This exercise will also help you sharpen your sense of dramatic transition, your ability to identify and express the moments at which relationships change and actions turn toward new objectives.

from

GOING TO POT

Georges Feydeau
Translated by Norman R. Shapiro

The scene is set in Maximilien Follavoine's study in the Follavoine apartment in Paris. Facing the audience is a large desk cluttered with folders, loose papers, and miscellaneous books, including an open dictionary. Among other furnishings, there is an armchair near the desk. Upstage center is a double door leading to the hall. Up right, a door leads to Madame Follavoine's bedroom.

Going to Pot is a farce based on the continual domestic strife between Maximilien and Julie Follavoine. The Follavoines are well-matched combatants. Neither will admit to any kind of error on his or her own part. Follavoine is chronically impatient, neat and formal, anxious to succeed. Julie is casual to the point of being unkempt. A few minutes before the opening of this excerpt, Julie had sent her maid to tell Follavoine that she wished to speak to him. Julie was too busy cleaning the bathroom to come to the study, so she was asking Follavoine to come to her. Follavoine became characteristically indignant at the request and sent the maid back to tell Julie that he was working and was too busy to leave his study. As the excerpt now begins, Follavoine is intently reading in the dictionary, annoyed and grumbling at his inability to find the word for which he has been searching. Julie enters in a huff.

(JULIE *enters in a flurry of agitation. She is dressed in a dirty bathrobe, with curlers in her hair and her stockings down around her ankles. A covered wash-bucket, full of water, is hanging from her arm.*)

JULIE. Well! Very nice! Too busy to speak to me!

FOLLAVOINE (*jumping at the sudden intrusion*). Julie! For God's sake, don't burst in here like that!

JULIE (*sarcastically*). Oh, I beg your pardon! Are you really too busy to speak to me . . . darling?

FOLLAVOINE (*angrily*). You're a fine one to talk! Why must *I* always come running? Why—

JULIE (*with an acid smile*). Of course. You're absolutely right. We're only married, after all!

FOLLAVOINE. So? What difference—

JULIE. Oh! If I were someone else's wife, I'm sure you could find the time—

FOLLAVOINE. All right! . . . That's enough! I'm busy!

JULIE (*putting down her bucket where she stands, center stage, and moving right*). Busy! He's busy! Isn't that fine!

FOLLAVOINE. Yes, that's what I said. Busy! (*Suddenly noticing* JULIE*'s bucket.*) What's that doing here?

JULIE. What?

FOLLAVOINE. Are you crazy, bringing your wash-bucket in here?

JULIE. Where? What wash-bucket?

FOLLAVOINE (*pointing to it*). That!

JULIE. Oh, that's nothing. (*As ingenuously as possible.*) It's just my dirty water.

FOLLAVOINE. And what am I supposed to do with it?

JULIE. It's not for you, silly. I'm going to empty it out.

FOLLAVOINE. In here?

JULIE. Of course not! What kind of a question . . . Do I usually empty my dirty water in your study? Really, I do have a little sense, you know.

FOLLAVOINE. Then why bring it in here in the first place?

JULIE. Because I just happened to have the bucket in my hand when Rose brought me your answer . . . your charming answer. (*Sarcastically.*) I didn't dare keep you waiting!

FOLLAVOINE. And you couldn't leave it outside the door?

JULIE (*becoming annoyed at* FOLLAVOINE*'s criticism*). Oh, for heaven's sake! If it bothers you so much it's your own fault. You shouldn't have said you were too busy to talk to me. Busy! I can just imagine! With what?

FOLLAVOINE (*grumbling*). With certain things—

JULIE. What things?

FOLLAVOINE. Certain things, I said . . . . I was looking up the Aleutian Islands in the dictionary. There! Now you know.

JULIE. The Aleutian Islands? The Aleutian . . . . Are you insane? You're going there I suppose?

FOLLAVOINE. No, I'm not going there!

JULIE (*sitting down on the sofa*). Then what difference could it possibly make where they are? Why does a porcelain manufacturer have to know about the Aleutian Islands, of all things?

FOLLAVOINE (*still grumbling*). If you think I give a damn! Believe me, if it was just for myself . . . But it's for Baby. He comes up with such questions! Children think their parents know everything. (*Imitating his son.*) "Daddy, where's the Aleutian Islands?" (*In his own voice.*) "Ha?" (*Baby's voice.*) "The Aleutians, Daddy, the Aleutians?" Believe me, I heard him the first time. The Aleutians . . . . How should I know where they are? You, do you know?

JULIE. Yes, I think . . . they're . . . I've seen them somewhere, on a map . . . but I don't remember exactly—

FOLLAVOINE. Ah! Just like me. But I couldn't tell Baby that I didn't remember exactly! What would he think of his father? So I tried to use my ingenuity. "Shame on you," I told him. "You shouldn't ask such questions. The Aleutians! That's not for children!"

JULIE. Ha ha! That's your ingenuity? What a stupid answer!

FOLLAVOINE. Unfortunately, it happens to be one of the questions in his geography lesson.

JULIE. Naturally!

FOLLAVOINE. Why do they have to keep teaching children geography nowadays! With railroads and boats that take you anywhere you want to go . . . . And with timetables that tell you everything—

JULIE. What? What has that got to do with it?

FOLLAVOINE. Just what I said. When you're looking for a city, who has to go running to a geography book? Just look at a timetable!

JULIE. And that's how you help your son? A lot of good that does him.

FOLLAVOINE. Well, damn it! What do you want from me? I did my best. I tried to look as if I really knew the answer but just didn't want to talk about it. So I said to him: "Look, if I tell you the answer, what good will it do you? It's better if you try to find it out for yourself. Later on, if you still want to know, I'll tell you." So I close the door and make a beeline for the dictionary to look it up. What do I find? Zero.

JULIE. Zero?

FOLLAVOINE. Nothing. Absolutely nothing.

JULIE (*skeptical*). In the dictionary? Let me have a look.

FOLLAVOINE. Sure, sure! Look to your heart's content! (JULIE *begins scanning the page.*) Really, you should have a talk with Baby's teacher. Tell her not to fill his head with things even grown-ups don't know . . . and that aren't in the dictionary.

JULIE (*suddenly looking up from the dictionary, with a sarcastic laugh*). Oh no! Ha ha ha! . . . Of all the stupid . . . Ha ha ha!

FOLLAVOINE. What's so funny?

JULIE. You've been looking under the E's!

FOLLAVOINE (*not quite understanding*). Well? Isn't it in the E's?

JULIE (*very condescending*). In the E's? The Aleutians? No wonder you couldn't find it!

FOLLAVOINE. All right then, if it's not in the E's, where is it?

JULIE (*turning to another page*). You'll see, you'll see . . . . "Illegible, illegitimate, ill-fated, ill-favored . . . ." Hm! (*Surprised.*) Now how did that happen?

FOLLAVOINE. What?

JULIE. It isn't there.

FOLLAVOINE (*triumphantly*). Aha! I told you, know-it-all!

JULIE (*embarrassed*). I don't understand. It should be between "illegitimate" and "ill-fated."

FOLLAVOINE. Maybe now you'll believe me when I tell you that dictionary is useless. You can look for a word under any letter you please, it's all the same. You'll never find the one you're looking for.

JULIE (*still staring at the open page*). I just don't understand—

FOLLAVOINE. That should teach you!

JULIE. Well at least I looked under the I's. That's a lot more logical than the E's.

FOLLAVOINE. Sure! "More logical than the E's." Ha ha! Why not the A's while you're at it?

JULIE. "The A's . . . the A's!" What are you talking about, "the A's!" (*She gradually changes her tone.*) The A's . . . . As a matter of fact, maybe . . . . Aleutians, Aleutians . . . . It seems to me . . . A . . . A . . . A . . . .

FOLLAVOINE (*imitating*). Ayayayayay!

JULIE (*scanning the columns quickly*). "Aleph, Aleppo, alert, Aleut . . . ." (*Triumphant.*) Aha! I've found it! "Aleutian Islands!"

FOLLAVOINE (*rushing to her side*). You've found it? You've found . . . (*In his haste he accidentally kicks* JULIE'*s bucket, which has been sitting on the floor since her entrance.*) Damn!

(FOLLAVOINE *picks up the bucket and, not knowing where to put it, places it on a corner of his desk.*)

JULIE. There, large as life: "Aleutian Islands, a chain of islands extending southward from Alaska, belonging to the United States."

FOLLAVOINE (*with a pleased expression, as if he had found it himself*). Fine, fine!

JULIE. And it even gives the area and the population: "1,461 square miles, 1,300 inhabitants."

FOLLAVOINE. Isn't that always the way! A minute ago we didn't know the first thing about them, and now we know more than we need. That's life!

JULIE. And to think we were looking under the E's and the I's.

FOLLAVOINE. We could have looked till doomsday.

JULIE (*picking up her bucket*). And all the time it was right there, in the A's.

FOLLAVOINE (*proudly*). Just like I said.

JULIE (*appalled*). You? Oh, now, just a moment! You said it . . . . Yes, you said it, but you didn't mean it.

FOLLAVOINE (*moving toward* JULIE). What are you talking about, I didn't mean it?

JULIE. Absolutely not! You were making fun of me. "Sure, why not the A's while you're at it?"

FOLLAVOINE. Now wait just a minute—

JULIE. It was at that very moment that I got a sudden vision of the word.

FOLLAVOINE. "Vision!" That's wonderful! She got a vision of the word! I tell her why not look in the A's, and suddenly she gets a vision! Just like a woman!

JULIE. Oh! That's too much! Really! Who took the dictionary and looked it up? Who, I ask you?

FOLLAVOINE (*sarcastically*). Sure, under the I's. Ha!

JULIE. Like you, looking in the E's! But who found it in the A's? Answer me that! Who?

FOLLAVOINE (*sitting down at his desk and raising his eyes to the ceiling in an offhand manner*). Very clever! After I tell you to look in the A's.

JULIE (*shaking the bucket furiously as she speaks*). Oh! You know perfectly well I found it! I found it! I—

FOLLAVOINE (*rushing to take the bucket from her*). All right! You found it! You found it! There, are you happy?

(*He looks on all sides for a place to put it.*)

JULIE. What are you looking for?

FOLLAVOINE (*sharply*). Nothing! Just some place to put this . . . this damned . . . .

JULIE. Well, put it on the floor!

FOLLAVOINE (*placing it on the floor, angrily*). There!

JULIE (*picking up the argument*). The nerve! To say that you found it when you know perfectly well that I—

FOLLAVOINE (*out of patience*). You're right! I admit it. You found it! You, you, you! All alone!

JULIE. Absolutely! And don't think you're doing me any favors either. Trying to tell me I didn't have a vision—

FOLLAVOINE. All right, all right! That's enough! Now, for God's sake, go get dressed. It's about time. Already eleven o'clock and you're still running around in that filthy bathrobe . . . .

JULIE. Of course! Change the subject!

FOLLAVOINE. Just look at yourself! Charming! Curlers in your hair, stockings down around your ankles . . .

JULIE (*pulling up her stockings*). And whose ankles should they be around? Yours? . . . There, I've fixed them. Are you happy?

FOLLAVOINE. Ha! If you think they'll stay up for more than half a minute the way you fixed them! It wouldn't kill you to wear garters, you know.

JULIE. And how am I supposed to attach them? I'm not wearing a corset.

FOLLAVOINE. Then go put one on, for God's sake! Who's stopping you?

JULIE. Why not? Maybe you'd like me to put on a hoopskirt just to clean the bathroom!

(*While speaking she has picked up the bucket and moved toward her room.*)

FOLLAVOINE. Well who the devil tells you to clean the bathroom in the first place? You have a maid, don't you? What on earth is she for?

JULIE (*returning in a huff and depositing the bucket at* FOLLAVOINE*'s feet*). I should let my maid clean the bathroom?

FOLLAVOINE (*moving off, stage right, to avoid another discussion*). Bah!

JULIE. Thank you just the same! Let her scratch and break everything? My mirrors, my bottles . . . . Oh no! I'd rather do it myself.

(*She sits in the armchair near the desk, casually resting one leg on the bucket, as if it were a footstool.*)

FOLLAVOINE. Then why, may I ask, do you have a maid if you won't let her do anything?

JULIE. She . . . She helps me.

FOLLAVOINE. Sure, sure she does. You do her work, and she helps you! How?

JULIE (*embarrassed*). She . . . well . . . she watches me.

FOLLAVOINE. Isn't that nice. She watches you. I pay the girl a salary like that just to stand and watch you. Lovely!

JULIE. Oh please! Don't talk about money all the time. It's so . . . so middle class!

FOLLAVOINE. Middle class! Middle . . . . Listen! I think when I give her such a salary I'm entitled to—

JULIE (*getting up and approaching* FOLLAVOINE). And besides, what are you complaining about? Do *I* get a salary? No. So, if it doesn't cost you any more, what's the difference who does the housework?

FOLLAVOINE. The difference . . . the difference is that I'm paying a maid to do the housework for my wife. I'm not paying a wife to do the housework for my maid. If that's how it is, we could do without the maid.

JULIE (*indignant*). Aha! I knew that's what you were getting at! I knew it! You begrudge me a maid!

FOLLAVOINE. Wait a minute! What are you talking about . . . . "begrudge you a maid"?

JULIE. Just what I said.

FOLLAVOINE (*out of replies, in desperation*). For God's sake, pull up your stockings!

JULIE (*angrily complying*). Oh! (*Picking up the argument.*) Such a fuss just because I like to clean the bathroom myself. (*She moves toward* FOLLAVOINE'*s desk, talking as she goes.*) I'm sure you're the first husband to criticize his wife for being a good housekeeper.

FOLLAVOINE. Now just a moment! There's a difference between being a good housekeeper and—

JULIE (*nervously arranging the papers spread over the desk*). I suppose you'd rather see me do like other women we know. Go out every day, spend all my time at the hairdresser's . . .

FOLLAVOINE (*seeing how* JULIE *is disturbing his papers*). What are you doing?

(*He rushes to the desk.*)

JULIE (*still on the same subject*). . . . at the dressmaker's . . .

FOLLAVOINE (*defending his papers as best he can*). Please!

JULIE. . . . at the races . . .

FOLLAVOINE. Please! For heaven's sake!

JULIE. . . . out in the morning, out at night, always running around, running around, spending your money . . . *your* money!

FOLLAVOINE. Will you please—

JULIE. A wonderful life you'd like me to lead.

FOLLAVOINE. . . . leave those papers alone! Leave them alone!

(*He pulls her away, stage left.*)

JULIE. Now what's the matter?

FOLLAVOINE (*trying to put his papers back in order*). My papers, damn it! That's what's the matter! Who asked you to touch them?

JULIE. I can't stand seeing such a mess.

FOLLAVOINE. Then look the other way. Just leave my papers alone!

JULIE. Your papers, your papers! If you think I care about your papers . . . .

(*She moves to leave, picking up her bucket as she passes.*)

FOLLAVOINE. Fine! Then prove it. Go putter around in your own room! (*Grumbling under his breath.*) Always fussing with something, always—

(*While speaking he sits down at his desk.*)

IMPROVISATIONS

There are often elements of pomposity and illogic in even the gravest human business. The way of farce is to spotlight that ridiculous side of our "serious" behavior. As for Follavoine and Julie, each believes that he or she is infallible, that his or hers is the right and only way, that the world, in effect, was made from his or her private blueprint. If events do not turn out as he or she thinks they ought to, the conclusion is that there is something wrong with reality or that the other person is in some way blamable. Thus, each party remains forever infallibly right, and the conflict begins another circle.

For an actor, creating humor is serious work. It requires a command of comedic techniques, a convincing characterization to support them, precise timing, and well-controlled pacing of the action in which the techniques are used. You must develop skill in such techniques as double takes, asides, pointing, and the uses of facial expressions to share secret information with the audience. You must be able to use a technique at the moment when it will have the greatest effect; if a moment too soon or late, the humor may be lost. You must be able to use the techniques to develop an action at a tempo which neither rushes nor drags, which neither confuses nor waters down the point of the action.

Follavoine, Julie. Basically, the humor of the excerpt develops from both characters being unwilling to admit any personal fault. Each has an attitude that says, "Events mean exactly what I choose for them to mean and will always mean exactly what I say they mean." Here is a theater game, called "Inside/Outside," which parallels the mental situation of the excerpt.

One of you imagines himself in an interior setting. The other imagines himself in an exterior setting. For examples, one might set himself in a phone booth in a hotel lobby, while the other establishes himself on a golf course on a warm day. Each proceeds to establish his imaginary environment by relating to it physically and using imaginary props. Each of you, however, is convinced that his own perception of where you are is the correct one, that his environment is the "real" one. In effect, two simultaneous realities are created, completely different from each other but occupying the same area. Your object is to cling to and maintain your own reality despite the constant incursions of your partner's reality, of his comments and actions. At the same time, your object is to prove to your partner that his perception of the environment is incorrect by reacting to his comments and actions as though they were taking place in *your* imaginary environment rather than his own. For example, one player might say to the other, "Move over; I can't putt with you standing in the middle of the green." The other might respond, "Would you loan me a dime? I have to call long distance, but I'm ten cents short."

This improvisation will help you develop a sense of the kind of business and movement essential to the humor of the conflict between Follavoine and Julie. Imagine that Follavoine is an artist. He is working on a very large landscape painting that he hopes to sell. He must move about as he works, for the painting is massive. At the same time, Julie is using him as a dressmaker's mannequin. He is wearing an unfinished evening gown on which Julie is attempting to make adjustments. Julie is enthralled with the prospect of how lovely she will look in her gown. Follavoine is occupied with thoughts of completing and selling his painting.

Another game, "One-upsmanship," has useful parallels to the action in the excerpt. Imagine that the two of you have a watermelon and are eating it in big slices. As you eat, you exchange outrageous insults. It is a kind of duel, each attempting to come up with a better put-down in response to his or her partner's insulting remark. Keep the exchange moving forward, building insult upon insult, rather than denying or defending them. But don't forget the watermelon. It was your original motive. Your principal concern throughout the improvisation is the chore of dealing with those big slices.

from

GOING TO POT

Georges Feydeau
Translated by Norman R. Shapiro

The scene is set in the study of the Follavoine apartment in Paris. With a couple slight exceptions, the furnishings are typical. Facing the audience is a large cluttered desk. On top of the desk is a porcelain chamber pot. Arranged about the room are a sofa, a couple chairs, and a cabinet with opaque glass panels. Inside the cabinet, unseen, there is another chamber pot. Upstage center, a double door leads to the hall. Up right, a door leads to Madame Follavoine's bedroom. (See page 50 for further background.)

Maximilien Follavoine is a porcelain manufacturer. He is hoping to become the exclusive supplier of chamber pots to the Army. When the present scene begins, Follavoine is alone in his study. He is waiting the arrival of M. Chouilloux, a representative from the War Ministry, who is coming to examine Follavoine's new unbreakable chamber pots. As he waits, Follavoine is seated at his desk, attempting to figure how much money he will make if his meeting with Chouilloux is a success. Julie, Follavoine's wife, suddenly enters, dressed in a dirty bathrobe and fallen stockings and with curlers in her hair. She is carrying a wash bucket full of dirty water. Chouilloux will enter soon. Also appearing briefly will be the maid, Rose.

JULIE (*still dressed as in the preceding scene, appearing suddenly in the doorway*). Maximilien, would you come here a minute.

FOLLAVOINE (*absorbed in his calculations*). Shhh! Can't you see I'm busy?

JULIE (*moving downstage, still carrying the bucket*). I'm asking you to come here a minute! Baby won't take his medicine.

FOLLAVOINE. Well then, make him take it! Show him who's boss! (*Suddenly noticing the bucket.*) Oh no!

JULIE. What?

FOLLAVOINE (*standing up*). Are you bringing that thing in here again?
JULIE. Well, I didn't have time to empty it yet. Now please, come and help me with—
FOLLAVOINE (*in a rage*). No, no, no! I've seen enough of that damned thing! Now get it out of here! Get it out of here!
JULIE. But I'm telling you that Baby—
FOLLAVOINE. I said get it out of here!
JULIE. But Baby—
FOLLAVOINE. I don't care! Get that thing out of here!
JULIE. But—
FOLLAVOINE. Out! Out! Out!
JULIE (*haughtily placing the bucket in the middle of the floor*). Now just you wait a minute! I'm sick and tired of hearing about my bucket!
FOLLAVOINE. What?
JULIE. That's all you can say: "Get it out of here! Get it out of here!" I'm not your maid, you know!
FOLLAVOINE (*unable to believe his ears*). I beg your pardon!
JULIE. You'd think I was supposed to do everything around here! If my bucket bothers you so much, you can get rid of it yourself!
FOLLAVOINE. Me?
JULIE. I brought it in, you can take it out.
FOLLAVOINE. But for God's sake! It's your dirty water, not mine!
JULIE. Well then, I give it to you. There! It's yours!
(*She moves off toward her room.*)
FOLLAVOINE (*following her and trying to catch her by the hem of her robe*). Julie! Are you out of your mind? Julie!
JULIE. It's yours, I said! It's all yours!
(*She runs into her room.*)
FOLLAVOINE. Julie! Get this thing out of here! Julie!
ROSE (*entering suddenly from the hall and presenting* MONSIEUR CHOUILLOUX, *a very well-dressed and distinguished gentleman*). Monsieur Chouilloux.
FOLLAVOINE. Get this thing—
CHOUILLOUX. Good afternoon, my friend.
FOLLAVOINE (*still at* JULIE*'s door, without turning around*). Oh shut up! (*He turns around suddenly, as* ROSE *leaves, and recognizes* CHOUILLOUX.) Monsieur Chouilloux! Oh! Monsieur Chouilloux, I didn't realize . . . I . . . . Oh! Please excuse me!
CHOUILLOUX. Am I a little early?
FOLLAVOINE. No, no . . . not at all. I . . . I was just speaking to my wife. I . . . I didn't hear you ring.
CHOUILLOUX. Oh, but I did ring. And the young lady let me in. (*Trying to be funny.*) I don't walk through the walls, you know!

FOLLAVOINE (*obsequiously*). Ha ha ha! Very good! Very good!

CHOUILLOUX (*modestly*). Well, really—

FOLLAVOINE (*hurrying to take his hat*). Here . . . I'll take that.

CHOUILLOUX. Much obliged. (*He moves downstage and stops short, amazed at the sight of* JULIE'*s bucket.*) My word!

FOLLAVOINE (*putting the hat on one of the cabinets, then dashing downstage to place himself between* CHOUILLOUX *and the bucket*). Oh, I beg your pardon! I . . . this . . . my . . . my wife was here a moment ago and . . . and this . . . she must have forgotten this . . . this . . . Rose! Rose!

ROSE'S VOICE. Yes, Monsieur.

FOLLAVOINE. Come in here! (*To* CHOUILLOUX.) Really, I don't know what to say. Especially at a time when I have the honor . . . the great honor . . . .

CHOUILLOUX (*bowing quickly several times*). Oh, please! Please—

FOLLAVOINE (*bowing in emulation of* CHOUILLOUX). Oh, but it is! It is an honor, Monsieur Chouilloux! A great honor!

CHOUILLOUX. Too kind! Much too kind!

ROSE (*appearing at the door*). You called, Monsieur?

FOLLAVOINE. Yes. Take Madame's bucket out of here, will you?

ROSE (*surprised*). Oh! Whatever is it doing in here?

FOLLAVOINE. She . . . she left it. By mistake.

ROSE. Oh my! She must be looking high and low for it. (*She picks it up.*)

FOLLAVOINE. That's right! Now go take it to her. And while you're there, tell her Monsieur Chouilloux is here.

ROSE. Yes, Monsieur. (*She leaves.*)

CHOUILLOUX. Please, don't trouble her on my account.

FOLLAVOINE. It's no trouble at all. If I don't hurry her a little . . . . You know how women are. Never ready!

CHOUILLOUX. Ah! Believe me, I can hardly say the same for Madame Chouilloux. Every morning she gets up at the crack of dawn, always the first one up. She does a lot of hiking, you know. It's splendid exercise for her. Of course, at my age . . . I'm afraid that sort of thing is a little strenuous. She does have her cousin, though. She takes her exercise with him.

FOLLAVOINE (*trying to be agreeable*). Yes, yes! So I've been told.

CHOUILLOUX. Of course, that suits me fine.

FOLLAVOINE. Yes . . . it keeps it all in the family.

CHOUILLOUX. That's right. All in the family. And then too, it doesn't tire me out. (*They laugh. Turning to move upstage,* CHOUILLOUX *catches sight of the chamber pot on the desk.*) Ah! I see you've been working on our little venture.

FOLLAVOINE (*following him*). Yes, yes . . . .

CHOUILLOUX (*with conviction*). That's the chamber pot.

FOLLAVOINE. That's the . . . . Yes, yes! You recognized it?

CHOUILLOUX (*modestly*). Well . . . . (*Observing it carefully.*) You know, it doesn't look bad at all. Not bad at all. And you say it's made of unbreakable porcelain?

FOLLAVOINE. That's right. Absolutely unbreakable.

CHOUILLOUX. Fine! Of course, you understand this *is* the feature that especially attracts the undersecretary and myself.

FOLLAVOINE. Yes, yes . . . .

CHOUILLOUX. Because if it were just ordinary porcelain, you know, we really wouldn't be interested.

FOLLAVOINE. Oh no! I agree with you!

CHOUILLOUX. You just look at it and it breaks.

FOLLAVOINE. In no time at all.

CHOUILLOUX. It would be a waste of the government's money.

FOLLAVOINE. Absolutely! Whereas this one . . . . Just look! It's solid, it will never wear out. Here, take it, feel it. You're an expert.

CHOUILLOUX. Oh, not really!

FOLLAVOINE. Yes, you are! Here, feel how light it is.

CHOUILLOUX (*taking the pot and weighing it in his hand*). Why yes, you're right. Strange, it scarcely seems to weigh anything at all.

FOLLAVOINE. And feel how nice it is to touch. See? You could almost say it would be a pleasure . . . Well, you understand . . . . (*Changing his tone.*) Now of course, we can make it in white or in color. If you want, for the army . . . maybe with stripes. Blue, white and red.

CHOUILLOUX. Oh, I don't think so. That would be rather pretentious.

FOLLAVOINE. Yes, you're absolutely right. And it would be a needless expense.

CHOUILLOUX. At any rate, we have time to think about all that. (*Placing the pot on the table and approaching* FOLLAVOINE.) You know, we've had a look at some enamel samples too. They aren't bad either.

FOLLAVOINE. Oh! Monsieur Chouilloux! No, you don't mean that! You wouldn't consider enamel!

CHOUILLOUX. Why not?

FOLLAVOINE. Well really! It's not for my own personal interest. I leave that out of it entirely. But Monsieur Chouilloux . . . enamel? . . . It has such an unpleasant smell. And besides, it isn't nearly as clean as porcelain. Really, there's no comparison.

CHOUILLOUX. Of course, there are two sides to the—

FOLLAVOINE. Not to mention the question of health. Certainly you must know that most cases of appendicitis come from using enamel utensils.

CHOUILLOUX (*half laughing, half serious*). Well, as far as that goes, I don't think . . . considering the use they're going to be put to . . . .

FOLLAVOINE. Ah, but you never know! The youth today are so thoughtless! Just picture a few soldiers. They want to try out their new equipment . . . They mix up a big punch, piping hot. The heat cracks the enamel, a few chips fall into the punch. They drink, they swallow . . . . Well, you can imagine what I mean, can't you?

CHOUILLOUX (*still amused*). Not really! I assure you I never had the experience of drinking punch from a—

FOLLAVOINE. No! But you *were* in the army.

CHOUILLOUX. I'm afraid not. When I went for my physical examination they made me undress, and then someone said to me: "Your eyes are no good." That settled my military career then and there. I've been in the War Ministry ever since.

FOLLAVOINE. Oh? Well, anyway, Monsieur Chouilloux, take my word for it. No enamel! Take vulcanized rubber, if you must, or even celluloid. Of course, in the long run nothing is as good as porcelain. The only trouble is that it's generally too fragile. But once that's taken care of . . . Look, let me show you. (*He takes the pot from the table.*) You'll see how solid it is. (*He raises the pot in the air as if to throw it to the floor, then changes his mind.*) No! Here, with the rug, it wouldn't prove anything. But in there, in the hall, on the bare floor . . . Just watch! (*While talking he goes to open the door upstage center, then returns center stage beside* CHOUILLOUX, *still holding the pot.*) Over there, Monsieur Chouilloux, over there! (CHOUILLOUX *takes a few steps in that direction;* FOLLAVOINE *holds him back*). No, no. Stay right here but look over there! (FOLLAVOINE *prepares to hurl the pot.*) Watch closely now! (*He winds up to throw.*) One! Two! Three! (*He throws it through the doorway.*) There!

(*At the very moment he says "There!" the pot hits the floor and breaks into a thousand pieces. For a moment the two characters stand gazing in astonishment.*)[1]

CHOUILLOUX. It broke!

FOLLAVOINE. Hm!

CHOUILLOUX. It broke!

FOLLAVOINE. Yes . . . it . . . it broke.

CHOUILLOUX (*walking over to the door*). No, no doubt about it. It's not an optical illusion.

1. Author's note: Should the pot fail to break as it hits the floor—as has occasionally happened—the actor playing the role of Follavoine may simply say: "You see! Unbreakable! And you know, you can throw it as many times as you like. Just to prove it to you, watch: One! Two! Three! . . . There!" etc.

FOLLAVOINE (*joining him*). No . . . no . . . It broke all right. Funny, I don't understand it. That's the first time . . . . Believe me, it's the first time that ever happened.

CHOUILLOUX (*moving downstage*). Perhaps it hit a flaw.

FOLLAVOINE (*joining him*). Perhaps. That must be it. Of course! Anyway, it really doesn't matter. It just proves that . . . that . . . well, like they always say: "The exception proves the rule." Because I assure you, it never breaks. Never.

CHOUILLOUX. Never?

FOLLAVOINE. Never! . . . Well, all right, maybe one in a thousand.

CHOUILLOUX. Ah! One in a thousand.

FOLLAVOINE. Yes, and . . . and even then . . . . Look, I'll prove it to you. (*He goes to the same cabinet and takes out another pot.*) Here's another one. You'll see. We'll be able to throw it all over the place. You'll see. Forget about the first one. It wasn't baked right.

CHOUILLOUX. I see. It was half-baked.

FOLLAVOINE (*placing himself in the center of the stage, next to* CHOUILLOUX). There. Now watch. One! Two! (*Suddenly changing his mind.*) No, wait. Here. You throw this one yourself.

(*He hands the pot to* CHOUILLOUX.)

CHOUILLOUX. Me?

FOLLAVOINE. Certainly! That way you'll get a better idea.

CHOUILLOUX. Oh?

(FOLLAVOINE *moves off a little, stage left.* CHOUILLOUX *takes his place.*)

FOLLAVOINE. Go ahead!

CHOUILLOUX. All right. (*Swinging the pot.*) One! Two! (*He stops, obviously nervous.*)

FOLLAVOINE. Go on, go on! What's the matter?

CHOUILLOUX. Nothing. . . . It's just. . . . It's the first time I've ever bowled with a . . . with a . . . . I feel silly.

FOLLAVOINE. Go ahead! Don't be afraid. I assure you, one in a thousand.

CHOUILLOUX. One! Two! And three! (*He flings pot.*)

FOLLAVOINE. There!

(*Once again the pot breaks as it hits the floor. The two characters stand motionless, thunderstruck.*)

CHOUILLOUX (*walking to the door after a little while, to survey the damage*). It broke!

FOLLAVOINE (*joining him*). It broke! . . . It . . . it . . . I . . . .

CHOUILLOUX. Two in a thousand!

FOLLAVOINE. All right! Two in a thousand! Look, I just don't understand it. There must be something. . . . It must be the way we throw them. I know when my foreman throws them. . . . Never, absolutely never!

CHOUILLOUX. Never?

FOLLAVOINE. Never!

CHOUILLOUX (*sitting down on sofa while* FOLLAVOINE *shuts the door upstage center*). That's very interesting.

FOLLAVOINE (*sensing* CHOUILLOUX'*s doubt*). But . . . certainly you must be able to appreciate the difference between ordinary breakable porcelain and—

CHOUILLOUX. And unbreakable porcelain.

FOLLAVOINE. Yes! (*Sheepishly.*) Still, I can tell I haven't exactly convinced you.

CHOUILLOUX. Oh, but you have . . . you have! I understand perfectly. They're the very same pots. Only, instead of breaking, they don't break.

FOLLAVOINE. Exactly!

CHOUILLOUX. Very interesting.

IMPROVISATIONS

While the situation in *Going to Pot* is usually absurd and the characters' behavior ridiculous, you, as an actor, must respect your character's serious attitude toward the events. You must develop the character as a real person, not as a stereotype. That tension between the absurd and the serious is the main source of the scene's humor.

Follavoine, Chouilloux. The juxtaposition of incongruous objects and/or actions is one of the basic elements of comedy—grown men bowling with a chamberpot and taking it quite seriously, for an obvious example. Improvise an action, using imaginary props, in which the two of you are butlers. You are arranging a table for a very formal dinner party. However, instead of using the usual assortment of silver, china, crystal, etc., you will use objects found in a mechanic's toolbox—wrenches, screwdrivers, whatever. You must play the scene quite seriously. Refer to the tools by their common names—"hammer," "wrench," etc.; but handle them as though they were forks, crystal, etc. So, you might find yourselves in a serious discussion about where the screwdrivers should be placed in relation to the hammers.

Invent an action based on mistaken identity. It takes place in a psychiatrist's office. You, Chouilloux, are the psychiatrist. You are waiting for a patient, who, you have been told, impersonates people. You are going to take him to the hospital when he arrives. You, Follavoine, are an office machine repairman. You come into Chouilloux's office intending to fix the office equipment. But you have made a mistake and are at the wrong address.

You might find that the theater game "Inside/Outside" (see page 57) would be a useful exercise for developing this excerpt.

from

THREE MEN ON A HORSE

ACT 1, SCENE 1

John Cecil Holm

It is morning in Ozone Heights, New Jersey, where Erwin and Audrey Trowbridge live in a house on a street of nearly identical "development" houses. The scene is set in the Trowbridge living room. There are a front door and a stairway leading upstairs. A bridge table is set for breakfast in the living room, because the kitchen floor is freshly painted.

This excerpt is from the opening scene of the play. So far, only a brief sequence of events has occurred. Erwin was upstairs getting ready for work. In the living room, his wife Audrey was preparing to send one of Erwin's suits to the cleaner and discovered a little notebook in a pocket of the suit. Looking through the notebook, she was shocked and distressed at what she read there. So, with a quick glance up the stairs, Audrey stealthily went to the phone and called her brother Clarence, briefly and weepily asking him to come over for a minute.

When this excerpt begins, Audrey has just finished phoning Clarence. The audience does not yet know why the notebook upset Audrey. Erwin is still upstairs. Audrey is about twenty-five, Erwin probably just a little older. Clarence will appear in a little while.

(*Hangs up. Wipes tears away, blows nose, then calls.*) Erwin, breakfast is ready.

ERWIN (*upstairs*). All right, dear. (AUDREY *blows nose and looks straight ahead.* ERWIN *comes quickly down the stairs and into room. He is dressed, except for his necktie. He is the model little commuter.*) I thought of another verse while I was shaving. Darned good, too— (*Sits at table.*) What's the matter, dear, something get in your eye?

AUDREY. I'll be all right.

ERWIN. Gee, that's too bad. It's this dry spell we're having. Dust everywhere.

AUDREY. Better drink your coffee before it's too cold.

ERWIN (*sits*). Oh, yes. (*Starts eating. Pause.*)

AUDREY. You forgot your necktie.

ERWIN (*looks*). Necktie? So I have. Oh, I couldn't decide which tie to wear.

AUDREY. You need new ones, I guess.

ERWIN. No, no. I have plenty. Gee, I'm late— (*Looking at wrist watch.*)

AUDREY (*crossing to the table*). You told me you'd stay home from the office one day this week.

ERWIN. I know I did, sweetheart— But not today. How in the name of Heaven can I turn out sixty-seven Mother's day greetings?

AUDREY (*suddenly; hopefully*). You could write them in the country. We could go for a drive. (*Sits.*)

ERWIN. No, no. I know I couldn't. I've never been able to write in the country—the birds and the butterflies, distract me— (*Suddenly.*) —wait— (*Writing.*) "The birds and the butterflies send you a greeting. It's spring and today in mem'ry we're meeting." Mother's Day Number Eleven. Yes, that's all right—well, that's another one. I'll call that "To Mother on Mother's Day"— (*Starts gulping breakfast. She goes to window.*) What's the matter?

AUDREY. I'm expecting Clarence, that's all.

ERWIN. I wish you'd have him visit when I'm not here; he gets me upset—he laughs at me—calls me the poet of Dobbins Drive.

AUDREY. He doesn't understand. He's a business man.

ERWIN. Business man? Every time I look out the window, I see forty-six empty houses that he's built and can't sell. My greeting card verses are read from Asbury Park to Seattle, Washington.

AUDREY. Well, I'm not going to be happy in Ozone Heights—after today.

ERWIN (*looks*). Why, has something happened?

AUDREY. Yes—something has. Erwin—

ERWIN. I wish you wouldn't say Erwin in that tone of voice, Audrey. I know my name is Erwin, but it makes me feel whatever has happened has something to do with me.

AUDREY. It has

ERWIN. Why, Audrey—

AUDREY. I discovered it before you came down.

ERWIN. About me? (AUDREY *nods.*) Why—why what is it?

AUDREY. I'm going to wait until brother gets here.

ERWIN. Do you have to have him here to tell me what it is?

AUDREY. Yes . . . Erwin, you don't love me any more. (*Sits—cries.*)

ERWIN (*crosses right*). Why, Audrey, of course I love you. Maybe I don't walk up and say, "Audrey, I love you," every time I see you . . . (*Sits.*) but you know how I feel. Gosh, I don't know how other husbands act. But I always do the best I can and we seem to get along all right. If I've done anything that's wrong I'd rather have you tell me than tell your brother. (*Turns front.*) I wish you wouldn't start the day off like this. It's hard to write my verses if I'm in the wrong mood, you know that. Come on, dear, tell Erwin what it is so he can explain and get to the office. . . .

AUDREY. Well, this morning the man came for your blue suit—and I gave it to him.

ERWIN. Well . . . why are we so excited about it? You were the one who said it needed cleaning. (CLARENCE *enters room. Looks at tie-less collar on* ERWIN. CLARENCE *is about thirty-five. A small town business man. A check book, pen and pencil in his breast pocket and when the jacket is open we see several lodge emblems.*)

CLARENCE. Hello, sis—you look all upset. Has he been doing anything to you?

ERWIN. I haven't done a thing that I know of. I was just having breakfast. It's something about my suit. My blue suit. Audrey sent it out to be cleaned.

CLARENCE. You being funny?

ERWIN. Maybe you think it's funny. I don't. I should be at the office and my wife tells me I don't love her any more.

CLARENCE. What has that got to do with a blue suit?

AUDREY. I sent it out to be cleaned, and—(*Takes notebook from pocket and crosses to* CLARENCE.) I found this notebook in the coat pocket.

ERWIN. Oh, that book. Is that what upset you. . . .

AUDREY (*holds up hand; goes to* CLARENCE. *Flips pages through*). Look at those names . . . Shirley, May, Lena, Wee, Bambola, Nell McClatchy, Squeeze . . . not one or two, Clarence, but pages of them . . . look at those telephone numbers . . . Jamaica six-three-two-one. . . .

ERWIN (*as* AUDREY *returns to davenport.*) But darling!

CLARENCE. My gosh, say. What are you keeping . . . a harem?

ERWIN. Wait, dear. (*Meekly.*) I can explain. It's only a hobby.

AUDREY. Only a hobby. Oh— (*Sits; cries.*)

ERWIN. They're horses.

CLARENCE. Horses, huh—

AUDREY. Horses!

ERWIN. Horse racing.

CLARENCE. Oh, is that it?

ERWIN. Yes!

CLARENCE (*stalking toward* ERWIN). I always knew you had some secret vice. I was telling Audrey just the other day. . . .

ERWIN. I don't play them.

CLARENCE. Then what do you do?

ERWIN. I dope them out.

CLARENCE. For who? For what?

ERWIN. For fun. I do it on the bus on the way to the office to pass the time. Like some people do crosswords. . . .

CLARENCE. Oh, you do?

ERWIN. Yes—one day I came across a racing paper on the bus and I found out that the fellow who doped them out wasn't so good. So the next day I did it myself for fun . . . and I've been keeping track of them in that book.

AUDREY (*stands*). But Erwin, you haven't explained all these numbers.

ERWIN. Certainly I have, sweetheart. (*Takes the book.*) Listen, here, I wrote on one page Jamaica—six—that's the sixth race. And then two-three-one. The two, three, and one was in the order I thought the entries would finish. On this other page is the way they did finish. (*Turning page*).

CLARENCE (*looking at book*). You mean you guessed them right?

ERWIN (*like a little boy*). Sure.

AUDREY. But that doesn't explain this number. (*Looking at book.*) This eight ninety-six point fifty—

ERWIN. It isn't a number. That's what I made the week of January twentieth—at two dollars a bet. Eight hundred and ninety-six dollars and fifty cents.

AUDREY. You made that and never told me?

ERWIN. Only on paper, sweetheart. Oh, I'd never bet on a horse. You know we couldn't afford that. (*To* CLARENCE.) Look—in the back of the book is what I would have made on a four horse parlay, playing two dollars a day fourteen thousand dollars and fifty cents since January first. It's what you call mental betting.

CLARENCE (*looking in book; businesslike*). So you win on paper. (*Takes book.*)

ERWIN (*going back to his breakfast*). But I wouldn't bet on a horse with real money.

CLARENCE. But on paper with two dollar bets you've made a few thousand dollars. Suppose you did put two dollars on a horse? And the horse paid three to one . . . you would have six dollars besides the original two dollars you bet.

ERWIN. Yes. But suppose the horse didn't win, I'd be out two dollars. Two dollars is a lot of money to us, Clarence.

CLARENCE (*slowly as he crosses to fireplace*). But according to your little book here, you couldn't have picked many horses that lost or you wouldn't have run up those figures.

ERWIN. Oh! yes. I have. Now last Tuesday, going to town, I went through the entries in the morning paper and picked out horses one-two-three in all the races and the one I picked in the fourth race, fell down and finished out of the money and one lost his rider and three were scratched.

CLARENCE. How about the other horses?

ERWIN (*eating*). Oh, they finished all right.

CLARENCE. One-two-three?

ERWIN. One-two-three.

CLARENCE (*turning away*). How long have you been doing this, Erwin?

ERWIN. Only since the first of the year.

CLARENCE. Well, that's long enough.

ERWIN. That isn't very long—

CLARENCE. I mean that's long enough to sock it away.

ERWIN. Sock what away?

CLARENCE (*going to table*). Come on now, Erwin. I've been around. I can see through you.

ERWIN. I don't know what you mean, Clarence.

CLARENCE. How many savings accounts have you, Erwin?

ERWIN. You mean banks?

CLARENCE. Yes, banks.

ERWIN. Only one. The Bowery Savings Bank.

CLARENCE. How much you got in there?

ERWIN. It's down to twenty-two dollars now.

CLARENCE. Say, Erwin, you're as plain as pie to me. You've been playing the horses since January—you've won a pile of money—you don't want anyone to know about it—so what do you do? You cry poor. So we'll think you're broke.

ERWIN. I am broke.

CLARENCE. I'll bet you've got about six different bank accounts under "nom de plums."

AUDREY. Why Erwin—

ERWIN. But I haven't, honest, I wish I had.

CLARENCE (*sits*). Now listen—you might die tomorrow, Erwin, and nobody knows about those bank accounts but you. Think of Audrey.

ERWIN. But honest, Clarence, I haven't any money. I don't know how you can think up things like this. Gee—if I had a brain like yours, I'd write detective stories. I only do this for fun—it's just a hobby—like—like—like golf—or—or tropical fish.

CLARENCE. Is that the truth?

ERWIN. That's the truth, Clarence!

CLARENCE. Great grief, man. Why don't you bet?

ERWIN. That would spoil it all.

CLARENCE (*baffled*). Do you mean to tell me you can pick horses, that win every day, and be satisfied with paper profits?

ERWIN. Yes.

CLARENCE. Why?

ERWIN. Because I did bet once.

AUDREY. Why, when was that, Erwin?

ERWIN. Well, that was a long time ago . . . I guess it doesn't hurt to tell about it now. We'd only been married a little while. You wanted something and I wanted to get it for you . . . you said it was too expensive. . . .

CLARENCE. What happened to the horse?

ERWIN. Oh, he lost.

AUDREY. Oh.

ERWIN. He was a good horse, though. One of the fellows at the office showed me a telegram right from the jockey who was going to ride in the race, saying, "It's a sure thing and to play right on the nose. . . ." So I did. I took ten dollars out of my envelop. . . . That was the time I told you my pocket was picked—remember? I was only making thirty then—

CLARENCE. So you thought the race was fixed, huh?

ERWIN. I didn't know anything about that. But he sure was a good horse . . . maybe something went wrong. Just as the race was about to start . . . this horse broke the barrier and ran all the way around the track before they could catch him . . . so they brought him back to the post . . . when the race started he was so tired he just stayed there.

CLARENCE. How do you pick these horses, Erwin?

ERWIN. When I get on the bus, I just look through the entries and pick out ones I like. I guess you'd call it playing hunches.

CLARENCE. Just for the fun of it. I guess a lot of people do that. I'll bet you even know what's going to win today.

ERWIN. Sure. I figured it out last night on the bus coming home—but I only figured the first race—Brass Monkey—is going to win it.

CLARENCE. Brass Monkey—

ERWIN. Sure, he's a good horse.

AUDREY. I'm awfully sorry, Erwin, I suspected you of anything wrong.

ERWIN (*going to her*). That's all right, darling. I'd never do anything behind your back, you know that.

CLARENCE. But great grief, Erwin, you don't seem to have any initiative. No other man would have let a chance like that slip through his fingers . . . why don't you bet?

ERWIN (*turning*). I don't think it would be moral for me to bet—we haven't enough money—

CLARENCE. That's ridiculous—why don't you make some? I told you I'd give you a percentage if you sold one of my houses—

AUDREY. That's sweet of you, Clarence.

ERWIN. I don't think I could sell one. Maybe Audrey could. I don't like them. (*Turns and goes toward door.*)

CLARENCE. What do you mean you don't like them?

ERWIN. I don't like them, that's all, and I couldn't sell anything I don't like.

AUDREY (*rising*). What's wrong with them?

ERWIN (*trapped*). There isn't anything wrong with them exactly, but well—there is too much water in the cellar.

CLARENCE (*going to* ERWIN). Now I don't want any minor criticisms from you after that porch you tacked on the house—I built a beautiful row of houses all alike, and you tacked that thing on. You put this house out of step, you know that?

ERWIN. Now listen, Clarence— (*Changing his mind as* CLARENCE *turns.*) Never mind, I'm late. (*Starts.*)

AUDREY. Wait a minute, Erwin.

ERWIN. What's the matter, darling? I have to go to work.

AUDREY. Don't you think you ought to apologize to Clarence before you go?

ERWIN. Apologize? For what?

AUDREY. For being so rude.

ERWIN. Rude?

AUDREY. Yes. About the houses. Erwin!

ERWIN. Well, I apologize—but I don't like water in the cellar—I don't think it adds anything to a house. (*Buzzer rings.* ERWIN *opens door.*)

BOY. Number one Dobbins Drive?—

ERWIN. That's right.

BOY. Package for Mrs. Trowbridge. (*Handing* ERWIN *package.*)

ERWIN. There she is there. . . . (*Starts out.*)

BOY. C.O.D. forty-eight dollars.

ERWIN. What?

AUDREY. I bought some dresses, darling.

ERWIN. C.O.D. forty-eight dollars? How are we going to pay it—what made you do that?

CLARENCE. I told her she needed some decent clothes. That's why, and since I've found out a few things today, I guess I was right.

ERWIN. We can't afford it— (*To* BOY.) Take them back, son. (*Giving him package.*)

BOY. I can't take them back. They've been altered.

AUDREY. That's right, Erwin. It was a sale. They'd cost me sixty-five next week. I saved you seventeen dollars. Darling, you know I didn't have anything to wear.

ERWIN. Nothing to wear! All I seem to do is pay for dresses and hats . . . and my life insurance. (*Crosses to cabinet, takes out "House hold Budget Book." Looks through book.*)

CLARENCE. Don't yell at my sister like that.

ERWIN. Nothing to wear. (*Reads.*) Listen—Nineteen twenty-nine—six dresses—four hats—Nineteen thirty—seven dresses—five hats—Nineteen thirty-one, thirty-two, and thirty-three—eight, nine, and ten dresses and five, four, and eight hats respectively, altogether, that's forty dresses and thirty-two hats. I should be in the hat business instead of trying to get some place.

AUDREY. Darling, it does sound like a lot, I know, but that's since nineteen twenty-nine—some of those hats I couldn't wear because my hair was growing back and they didn't fit.

ERWIN. Here's my hat—five dollars it cost me in nineteen thirty-one and it's good enough for me, fall, winter, spring, and summer—(*Puts on hat.*) and look at it.

CLARENCE. Women's things are different—some women buy—

ERWIN. Well, look at it.

AUDREY. I'm looking. I have a right to have a dress or two. I've saved a little money from the budget and anyway how do I know you haven't been betting on the horses.

CLARENCE. Yes, there's a lot of things about you I'd like to know—

ERWIN. My gosh, don't I bring home my salary every week? You know I never bet on a horse or anything.

AUDREY (*going to* CLARENCE). Oh, Clarence, let's not argue any more—

CLARENCE (*enfolding* AUDREY). Don't worry Audrey. I'll pay for the dresses.

ERWIN. Oh, no you won't. I don't want you to pay for anything. (*Goes to cabinet, takes tobacco tin. He takes out bills.*) Here, this is for your dresses. This ten was going to be for a split bamboo weakfishing outfit. These three tens were going to be for a motor trip for the two of us and this ten was supposed to become a panama and a pair of sport shoes—but pay for the dresses. Don't forget to get a receipt. (*Picks up box and puts it back in cabinet.*)

AUDREY. Where are you going?

ERWIN. To the office—I'm late.

AUDREY. You've forgotten your necktie.

ERWIN. What's the difference. Who cares how I look? To Hell with the tie.

AUDREY. Erwin.

ERWIN. And to Hell with this house.

CLARENCE. What?

AUDREY. Erwin! You'll hurt Clarence's feelings.

ERWIN. And I won't apologize. (*Rushing past delivery boy and out door.*)

AUDREY (*calls*). Erwin.

IMPROVISATIONS

Throughout the play, people are continually attempting to see Erwin as someone other than himself, to cast him in roles for which he never auditioned. They are continually attempting to interpret his actions in such ways as to agree with their *own* wishes and fears. He is, in nearly everyone's fantasy, exactly what they want him to be; and nearly everyone, sooner or later, becomes angry with him for *not* being who they want him to be.

Audrey, Erwin, Clarence. The theater game "Who Am I?" (see page 21) is a good way of getting into the problems of Erwin's identity in relation to Audrey's and Clarence's expectations of him and of the shift of relationships when the third actor enters the scene. Each of you should get a turn in the Who-am-I role. When the game goes well, the kind of excitement created during it will carry over into your playing of the scene; for, playing comedy requires concentration, alert responses, and, simply, a great deal of constant energy.

This exercise can be useful for developing characterizations. Each of you selects an animal image which exemplifies the walk, the movements, and the general rhythm of your particular character. Next, the three of you proceed to move about the room, each in the physical manner of his or her chosen animal. As you move about, one of you calls out a specific locale, such as "submarine" or "supermarket" or "library." The three of you then improvise a scene which takes place in that setting. While retaining your external animal mannerisms, you are to play out the action as human characters, as Audrey, Erwin, and Clarence—in effect, as human minds and spirits in animal bodies.

You will probably find that this exercise will help give you a mental fix on your character, a metaphor that you can use as a focus for your characterization. The metaphors "stealthy as a fox" or "proud as a peacock," for examples, become real experiences, the memories of which can be carried over when you begin working with the script of the excerpt. The patterns of gesture and movement you explore in this sort of exercise are particularly appropriate to comedy, in which character "types" are often an important element.

Audrey, Clarence. Suppose that Clarence is Audrey's father, rather than her brother. (In a sense, that is another dimension of their relationship in the excerpt.) Audrey is not yet married to Erwin. But she is planning to elope with him very soon. The pair must elope, because Clarence despises Erwin and has banned him from his, Clarence's, house. Now, improvise a scene in which the two of you, Audrey and Clarence, are playing ping pong. Clarence announces that he has a surprise for Audrey: he has bought two tickets on a world cruise for Audrey and himself. (Naturally, he bought them with money from an inheritance that belongs to Audrey.) That will put Audrey in a conflict. On one hand, she wants to go through with her plan to elope with Erwin. On the other, she does not want to hurt Clarence's feelings by declining to go on the cruise with him.

Erwin, Gamblers. Erwin is not a gambler. He does not actually bet on horse races. He plays the horses only in his mind, as a hobby. He does, however, have an obvious great gift for picking winners. Later in the play, he will meet some real, professional horse players. Before you read the entire play, try improvising a scene in which Erwin meets some real race track gamblers. Then, compare the way you have developed the situation with the way it is developed in the script.

Remember that at the center of your improvisation is the fact that Erwin is but a gifted hobbyist, while the gamblers earn their very livings from the horses. That will be the basis of the relationship among you. That is, one side, either Erwin or the gamblers, will have to discover some information about the other, information which he finds in some way attractive or potentially "useful" and wants to pursue. Remember, too, that your improvisation must have a definite setting. The setting you choose can drastically affect how your encounter begins and develops. Consider, for example, the different limitations of an elevator, a city park, and a tavern.

The game "Inside/Outside" is appropriate to this excerpt. You might try it with Audrey and Clarence, together, relating to one reality (setting) and Erwin to another.

from

HOLIDAY

ACT 2

Philip Barry

It is a few minutes to midnight, New Year's Eve. The scene is set in what was once the childrens' playroom on the fourth floor of the Seton house on Fifth Avenue, New York City. The children are grown, but the storybook decorations and small-scale furniture of the room have remained unchanged over the years. There is an old-fashioned music box. Against a wall, a table has been set for a small supper party with sandwiches and champagne. To the rear is a door that leads downstairs, where a large party is progressing.

Johnny Case is thirty years old but has had the responsibilities of an adult since he was ten. An orphan, he had worked ceaselessly to support himself and then to put himself through law school as well. In becoming a lawyer, his plan had been to accumulate quickly enough money to be able to quit working, at least for awhile, and find out what he really would like to do with his life.

Julia Seton is twenty-eight. She is beautiful. Her family are *the* Setons, wealthy, stodgily conservative, listed in the social register. Julia first met Johnny Case while vacationing alone at Lake Placid. In that romantic setting, away from her father's influence, she had been charmed by Johnny's fresh optimism, and the pair were quickly engaged. But it was not long after having returned to her father's house that Julia also returned to her father's narrow way of thinking. By the time of the present excerpt, what had originally seemed charming about Johnny's attitudes toward money and success, has come to seem irresponsible and improper to Julia.

The excerpt takes place on the night of Julia's and Johnny's engagement party, which is being given by Julia's father. It is a great, dull affair, one of the season's important social events, to which all the very best people have been invited. Just before the excerpt begins, Johnny unexpectedly learned that he had suddenly made a large amount of money on the stock market. In his excitement, he proceeded to tell Julia's father about his plan to retire for awhile.

Seton, of course, was appalled; such a scheme is contrary to everything the Setons stand for. As the excerpt now opens, Seton has just gone off in a huff to return to his guests, leaving Julia with Johnny. Midway in the excerpt, Linda Seton will appear.

Linda is Julia's sister. But she is so unlike Julia that it is hard to believe that the two are related. Linda is twenty-seven but looks twenty-two. Rather than beautiful, she is very pretty. She is vivacious, adventurous, and likes people, accepting them entirely as they are. She is, in fact, much like Johnny Case, whom she has loved since the day she met him. Earlier this evening, unable to stomach her father's and sister's pomposity, she had bolted the grand party. It was she who had then had the table set up in the playroom, planning an intimate New Year's get-together for a few friends, a sort of countermeasure to the goings-on below. But, sadly, all her guests were waylaid downstairs.

JOHNNY (*still hopeful, turns to* JULIA). —Darling, he didn't get what I'm driving at, at all! My plan is—

JULIA. Oh, Johnny, Johnny, why did you do it?

JOHNNY. Do what?

JULIA. You knew how all that talk would antagonize him.

JOHNNY (*a moment*). You think talk was all it was?

JULIA. I think it was less than that! I'm furious with you.

JOHNNY. It wasn't just talk, Julia.

JULIA. Well, if you think you can persuade me that a man of your energy and your ability *could* quit for *any* length of time, you're mistaken.

JOHNNY. I'd like to try it.

JULIA. It's ridiculous—and why you chose tonight of all nights to go on that way to Father—

JOHNNY. Wait a minute, dear: we'd better get clear on this—

JULIA. I'm clear on it now! If you're tired, and need a holiday, we'll have it. We'll take two months instead of one, if you like. We'll—

JOHNNY. That wouldn't settle anything.

JULIA. Johnny, I've known quite a few men who don't work—and of all the footling, unhappy existences—it's inconceivable that you could stand it—it's unthinkable you could!

JOHNNY. —I might do it differently.

JULIA. Differently!

JOHNNY (*a moment, then*). You—you have a great time standing me against a wall and throwing knives around me, don't you? (*In an instant he has taken her in his arms.*)

JULIA (*against his shoulder*). What do you do things like that for? What's the matter with you, anyway?

JOHNNY (*he stands off and looks at her*). Haven't you the remotest idea of what I'm after? (*She looks at him, startled.*) I'm after—all that's in me, all I am. I want to get it out—where I can look at it, know it. That takes time. —Can't you understand that?

JULIA. But you haven't any idea yet of how exciting *business* can be—you're just beginning! Oh, Johnny, see it through! You'll love it. I know you will. There's no such thrill in the world as making money. It's the most—what are you staring at?

JOHNNY. Your face.

JULIA (*she turns away*). Oh—you won't listen to me—you won't hear me—

JOHNNY. Yes, I will.

JULIA (*a pause. Then* JULIA *speaks in another voice*). And you'd expect me to live on—this money you've made, too, would you?

JOHNNY. Why, of course not. You have all you'll ever need for anything you'd want, haven't you?

JULIA (*another pause, then*). —I suppose it doesn't occur to you how badly it would *look* for you to stop now, does it—?

JOHNNY. Look? How? (*She does not answer.*) —Oh—you mean there'd be those who'd think I'd married money and called it a day—

JULIA. There would be. There'd be plenty of them.

JOHNNY. —And you'd mind that, would you?

JULIA. Well, I'm not precisely anxious to have it thought of you.

JOHNNY. —Because *I* shouldn't mind it—and I think that lookout's mine. Oh, darling, you don't see what I'm aiming at, either—but try a little blind faith for a while, won't you? Come along with me—

JULIA. Johnny— (*She reaches for his hand.*)

JOHNNY. —The whole way, dear.

JULIA. —Wait till next year—or two years, and we'll think about it again. If it's right, it can be done, then as well as now. —You can do that for me—for us—can't you? (*A moment. Then he slowly brings her around and looks into her eyes.*)

JOHNNY. You think by then I'd have "come around"—that's what you think, isn't it?—I'd have "come around"—

JULIA. But surely you can at least see that if—! (*She stops, as* LINDA *re-enters.*)

LINDA. It lacks six minutes of the New Year, if anyone's interested. (*A moment, then* JULIA *moves toward the door.*)

JULIA. Come on, Johnny.

JOHNNY (*to* LINDA). Where are the others?

LINDA. My pretty new friends? Well, it seems they've ditched me. (*She starts a tune on the music box.*) —*This* won't make too much noise, do you think?

JOHNNY. How do you mean, Linda?

LINDA. I imagine Peter and Mary got tired of being put through their tricks, and slid out when they could. Nick and Susan left a message upstairs with Delia[1] saying that they had to go after them. I'm supposed to follow, but I don't think I will, somehow.

JULIA. Oh, I *am* sorry.

LINDA. Are you, Julia? That's a help. (*She goes to the supper table.*) —Anyone care for a few cold cuts before the fun starts?

JOHNNY. You're not going to stay up here all alone—

LINDA. Why not? I'm just full of resources. I crack all kinds of jokes with myself—and they say the food's good. (*She takes a bite of a sandwich and puts it down again.*) Ugh! Kiki—

JULIA. Linda, this is plain stubbornness, and you know it.

LINDA (*wheels about sharply*). Listen, Julia—! (*She stops and turns away.*) No—that gets you nowhere, doesn't it?

JULIA (*to* JOHNNY). Are you coming?

JOHNNY. —In a moment, Julia. (JULIA *looks at him. He meets her gaze steadily. She turns and goes out. There is a pause, then:*)

LINDA. You'd better run on down, don't you think?

JOHNNY. Not right away. (*Another pause.*)

LINDA. I'm afraid I don't know how to entertain you. I've done all my stuff.

JOHNNY. I don't need entertaining.

LINDA (*another pause, a very long one.* LINDA *looks uncertainly toward the music box; finally*). —You wouldn't care to step into a waltz, Mr. Case?

JOHNNY. I'd love it. (*She extends her arms. He takes her in his. They begin to waltz slowly to the music box.*)

---

1. Delia is the maid. The others are the friends whom Linda had invited to her supper, but who had not gotten past the "official" party below.

IMPROVISATIONS

To respect is to love. Mutual respect is the first condition of a healthy relationship between two people. Neither must try to dictate the other's life. Each must accept the other's freedom to dictate his or her own life, to do and be what his or her own needs and aversions dictate. Clearly, in the excerpt from *Holiday*, Julia is incapable of respect, of accepting Johnny solely for who he is. Linda, on the other hand. . . .

Julia, Johnny. For several months now, you have believed yourselves to be in love. You have just spent an evening at a benefit party at Julia's father's country club. In the course of the evening you had some sort of tiff, which revealed to both of you, for the first time in your relationship, that there are some very basic differences in your opinions. Improvise a scene in which you are now driving home from the party. You are furious with each other and conversation is difficult. Further, Julia is a heavy smoker, and Johnny has been carrying her cigarettes for her all evening. It is raining, and you are lost in a remote part of the countryside.

Julia is a character governed by, and incapable of going against, social and family expectations; they are a pressure within her demanding that she behave properly and correctly, as a woman of her social class "ought" to. At the same time, there is also within her the pressure of her desire to have Johnny Case. Under the circumstances in the play, those two inner pressures are incompatible. That is one of the main problems in developing the parts of Julia and Johnny. As Julia, you must create a character whose way is to try to go along with *both* pressures, to get both the worlds she wants. As Johnny, then, you must be able to deal with someone who is capable of dissembling, of creating a false appearance by leaving out important facts about herself. At the same time, you must create a character who, through most of the play, is so in love that he is unable even to suspect that his fiancee is capable of dishonesty.

Suppose the two of you had become engaged, but that Johnny had soon been recalled to combat flight duty by the Air Force. He became a well-known hero. Then, his plane was shot down in a remote area, and he was reported missing in action. But, as it turned out, he had survived, and after great hardship and more heroism he returned to civilization. Improvise a scene in which Johnny returns to his home town and is received with a hero's welcome at the airport. Julia is there to greet him. He does not know that she had married someone else during his absence. Johnny still wants to get married. Julia wants to maintain appearances, to properly greet the returning hero as her social position demands. She does not want to reveal to him that she is married.

Linda, Julia. In the excerpt, both female characters are under considerable stress. Each is in turmoil within, in contrast to the luxury of their external setting.

Improvise a scene which takes place at poolside on the Setons' country estate. Julia has secret doubts about whether the differences between herself and Johnny can be overcome. Linda perceives Julia's doubts and proceeds to try to convince her that she should marry Johnny despite the differences in their social and economic backgrounds. But Julia does not want to admit, even to her sister, that anything could possibly be wrong. She wants to maintain an appearance that all is just as it should be. So, Julia must take opposition to Linda's attempts to convince and reassure her, implying to Linda, for example, that she is simply being nosy and is interfering unnecessarily. Finally, all the time she is persuading Julia, Linda herself is secretly in love with Johnny. Thus, each of you has an inner conflict she does not want revealed.

Suppose Julia and Linda are in their teens. The two of you are staying with friends for the summer. Linda has been invited to go sailing and has promised her friends that she will meet them without fail at the yacht basin. Improvise a scene in which Linda discovers that she has left her sailing clothes at home. She wants to borrow an outfit from Julia. Julia, however, does not want to loan her the outfit, even though she has no need of it herself. Secretly, Julia is jealous of Linda and afraid that Linda will be more attractive than she.

Courtesy of Columbia Pictures. Johnny (Cary Grant) and Linda (Katharine Hepburn) in the play room, from the 1938 film *HOLIDAY*.

Courtesy of Columbia Pictures. Linda (Katharine Hepburn) watches Johnny (Cary Grant) kiss her sister Julia (Dorris Nolan). Linda loves Johnny and they'd make a better pair. Johnny is engaged to marry Julia. 1938 film version of Philip Barry's play *HOLIDAY*.

Courtesy of Pathé Pictures. (Left to right) Ann Harding, Edward Everett Horton and Mary Astor. Ann Harding has received an Oscar nomination for her role in the 1930 film version of Philip Barry's play *HOLIDAY*.

3

A Resource Book

Suggested improvisations for scenes in

SCENES FOR ACTING AND DIRECTING, Vol. 1

SCENES FOR ACTING AND DIRECTING, Vol. 2

SCENES FOR ACTING AND DIRECTING, Vol. 3

SCENES FOR ACTING AND DIRECTING, VOL. 1

ALL MY SONS page 1
Ann. Imagine a sort of prelude to the excerpt. It is the day after your arrival at the Keller home. it is early morning. You come out of the house into the back yard. Improvise actions by which you establish the fact that you are outdoors. Remember that it is a setting which you had once known well, and you are seeing it again for the first time in several years.

Chris. Consider the events and emotional changes which Chris describes in his long speech (beginning at the bottom of page 3). Imagine that it is a time in the past. You, Chris, have recently returned from the War and have taken a job in your father's business. You are just now returning home after your first day on the job. No one else is home at the moment. Improvise a brief scene in which your actions suggest your state of mind, your feelings about what you might have experienced today.

Ann, Chris. Suppose that when the excerpt opens, Chris's father has just gone into the house to prepare a round of iced tea. This is the first opportunity you have had to talk privately since Ann's arrival, and you cannot be sure of getting another. You know that Joe will be returning at any moment. You must make every word and gesture count; you must express your feelings and thoughts as clearly and briefly as possible, perhaps in as few as three or four improvised lines or short speeches apiece.

Ann, Chris. Suppose that when the excerpt opens, Mrs. Keller is seated just inside the back door. Her back is to you, but you are still within range of her hearing. Just as in the excerpt, each of you is anxious to learn what the other feels toward you, you want to know exactly where the two of you stand. That is the whole point of Ann's visit. How, then, will you attempt to overcome the obstacle of Mrs. Keller's nearness and get matters clear between you?

ALL MY SONS page 5
Keller, Deever. Improvise a flashback scene in Keller's factory, in which the two of you first discover the cracked cylinder heads on the aircraft engines you have been manufacturing for the military.

Keller, Mechanic. It is a week after Keller first learned of the cracked cylinder heads. One of his employees, a mechanic, has just now also discovered the defect. Improvise a scene in which the mechanic, unaware that Keller already knows, comes to Keller's office to tell him of the defective parts. Keller is studying some reports and is unwilling to be disturbed.

DEEP ARE THE ROOTS page 8

Brett, Alice, Bella, Howard. Improvise a scene which could have occurred prior to the excerpt in *Scenes for Acting and Directing Vol. 1.* Brett is just getting off a train, returning home from the War, a hero. Bella, Alice, and Howard have come to meet him. You might also improvise a scene in which Brett has returned unannounced. Alice, Howard, and Bella are in the living room of Alice's house when Brett arrives at the door.

Brett, Alice, Howard, Bella. Locking arms at the elbows, Alice, Howard, and Bella closely encircle Brett. The point is to make Brett feel trapped, to "suffocate" him with confinement. Brett, without using his hands, attempts to break out of the circle. The captors might simultaneously try to convince Brett to give up struggling, each reasoning in her or his particular manner.

Alice, Brett. Imagine that it is now five years after the time of the excerpt in *Scenes for Acting and Directing Vol. 1.* The two of you, not having seen each other for five years, meet by chance in a large Northern city. Improvise your meeting, first, in an elegant restaurant, then, in a fast service cafeteria.

AH! WILDERNESS page 15

Richard. In his long opening speech, Richard, his mind anxious and excited, seems to skip randomly among a variety of topics. Imagine that it is now twenty years later. You, Richard, are in a much calmer frame of mind and reminiscing about your boyhood. Improvise a monologue in which you recall your visit to Pleasant Beach House, your meeting with Muriel the next night, and your feelings about those events. Or you might imagine that you are preparing notes for a personal memoir. Tape record your reminiscences. You will probably find it interesting to listen to the tape afterward.

Muriel, Richard, Second Boyfriend. Suppose it is some time in the past, before Richard and Muriel have been forbidden to meet. Improvise a scene in which Richard has come to Muriel's house to ask her to go to a dance with him. It would be the first time he has asked her to go out with him. They are alone in the back yard. This situation in itself can be an interesting improvisation. However, you might try a complication. After Richard and Muriel have been together a brief while, a second young man enters. He is about Richard's age, selfconfident, the captain of the school football and debating teams. He, too, has come to ask Muriel to the dance.

Muriel. You have just parted abruptly from Dick (the climax to the excerpt) and are walking home. Improvise a monologue in which you are thinking aloud about what has just occurred and about your feelings toward Dick.

THE CHALK GARDEN page 25

Laurel, Maitland. Shortly after Maitland has become Laurel's governess, she and

Laurel go for a walk in a park. Walking not very far from them is another person. Laurel recognizes the person as an old family friend. Maitland also recognizes the person, but as someone who knows that she had been in prison. Improvise a scene in which Laurel attempts to convince Maitland that they should approach this person.

THE CHALK GARDEN page 30
Mrs. St. Maugham, Olivia. Imagine that it is a time in the past, and that Olivia is engaged to be married for the first time. Improvise a scene in which the two of you are discussing plans for the wedding. You are dusting the room, reporting plants, or performing some other domestic task as you talk. Your attitudes toward the coming event, toward Olivia's fiancé, and toward each other should be based on evidence in the excerpt.

THE LITTLE FOXES page 36
Regina, Horace. Improvise a new ending for the excerpt, one in which Horace is able to reach a spare bottle of medicine just in time to prevent his collapse.

THE LITTLE FOXES page 42
Alexandra, Regina. Regina is sitting in the living room knitting when Alexandra enters to tell her mother that she is going to leave home. (Her feelings toward Regina and her reasons for wanting to leave are the same as those she expresses in the excerpt in *Scenes for Acting and Directing Vol. 1.)* However, throughout the improvisation, Regina's interest is wholly occupied by her knitting. She does not look at Alexandra and responds to her only in a disinterested, though not unpleasant, manner. A typical response from Regina might be: "That's nice, dear."

You might then reverse the situation. Alexandra is playing solitaire when she tells her mother that she plans to leave home tomorrow. Regina might be knitting, or perhaps she has just entered the room. She reacts to Alexandra's news as she normally would (from what you know about her from the excerpt). But this time it is Alexandra who treats the matter in a light, pleasantly conversational manner.

LADIES IN RETIREMENT page 46
Ellen, Louisa, Emily, Leonora. The four of you play the game Two-way Conversation (see page 11 of this book). Ellen is in the middle. Leonora is on one side of her, Louisa and Emily are on the other. Leonora attempts to convince Ellen that Louisa and Emily must leave immediately, while the two sisters attempt to persuade Ellen that she must get rid of Leonora. Ellen, of course, attempts to mollify both sides. A variation of this would be for Ellen to be planning the menu for dinner. Leonora, on one side, demands that they have roast beef. Louisa and Emily, on the other side, demand pork chops, for example. Both sides are adamant. Ellen attempts to compromise with each.

LADIES IN RETIREMENT page 52

Albert, Ellen. Ellen has what Albert wants: the means of helping him hide from the police. But Albert also has something subtle which Ellen wants: his knowledge. She would be more comfortable knowing to what extent he is bluffing with his sly insinuations about Miss Fiske's absence. The conflict between them is an elaborate game of You Have It, I Want It. You can simplify and get a closer feeling of the conflict by playing the game as it is described on page 20 of this book. Play the game, first, imagining that Albert wants what Ellen has. Then, reverse roles: Albert has what Ellen wants.

STAGE DOOR pages 58and 63

Terry, Jean. Improvise a scene in which Terry comes into the bedroom in the Footlights Club and tells Jean that she, *Terry,* has been offered a movie contract. Unlike the excerpt in *Scenes for Acting and Directing Vol. 1,* Jean has not been included in the contract deal.

A RAISIN IN THE SUN page 67

Ruth, Beneatha, Mama. Imagine that it is late on a stormy night. The three of you have just arrived in this large city where you plan to make your home. You have no friends here. It has been a long, wearisome train journey. Ruth is ill and needs assistance. Improvise a scene in which both Mama and Beneatha have definite ideas about what should be done for Ruth, but they do not agree with each other, and each strives for control of the situation. Remember that Ruth, too, must work into the scene.

A RAISIN IN THE SUN page 75

Beneatha, Asagai. Imagine that you are at a college dance. You meet for the first time during an intermission. Beneatha had come to the dance with George Murchison, but Asagai wants to take her home.

THE OLD MAID page 81

Charlotte, Delia. Imagine that it is the day before Delia's wedding. A few minutes ago, Clem Spender arrived to talk to Charlotte. But to keep Delia from meeting him, Charlotte had to hide Clem quickly. Improvise a scene in which Charlotte is now helping Delia pack for her honeymoon. Clem is in an adjacent room. Charlotte must attempt to keep Delia from entering the room in which Clem is hidden.

Charlotte and Delia would be well suited for a game of You Have It, I Want It (as described on page 20). Charlotte wants what Delia has.

THIEVES' CARNIVAL pages 85 and 88

Gustave, Juliette. Gustave has accidentally broken a large piece from a valuable vase belonging to Lady Hurf. He does not want Juliette to know of the damage. Improvise a scene in which Gustave tries to shield the vase from Juliette's view. At the same time, Juliette attempts to persuade him to go into the garden with her to watch the sunset.

Gustave, Chief Mechanic. Suppose that you, Gustave, have taken a job as an auto mechanic. Actually, you know nothing at all about automobiles and have never even driven one. But you sorely needed a job. Improvise a scene in which the foreman of the garage requires you to help him diagnose a faulty engine.

EDWARD, MY SON page 95

Evelyn, Arnold. Suppose that Edward was arrested for an alleged involvement with illegal drugs. His trial has just taken place, and the judge has retired to his chambers to consider a verdict. Improvise *in silence* a scene in which the two of you are in an otherwise empty courtroom, waiting for the judge to return with his verdict. (Consider the conflicting thoughts and feelings any parents might have in such a situation: protective, angry; hopeful, depressed; accusing, self-accusing; united, apart; etc.)

Evelyn, Arnold. Each of you holds an end of the same rope (a real, not imaginary, rope). Imagine that this rope is the line of communication between you and your mate, your only "voice." Through it you can express all your feelings toward your mate, and your mate can express his or her reactions toward you. At first the rope lies limp between the two of you. One of you might then begin the "conversation" with a gentle, questioning tug or perhaps with an abrupt jerk. At times you may engage in a strenuous tug-of-war, neither willing to give in. You may "snap" at each other. Or one may try to pull the other closer...and so on.

Evelyn, Arnold. Imagine that it is a time in the past, when Edward is a small child. In the past month, Arnold has given the boy eight or nine very expensive toys. Improvise a scene in which Arnold comes home bearing yet another, such toy. Evelyn is in the living room when Arnold enters with the package.

THE ENCHANTED page 102

Supervisor. Present a common object (a real prop) to the rest of the group. The object might be an apple, a hat, a piece of paper from the waste basket, or a chair, for examples. Describe the object, improvising a unique history for it or a speech of praise for its unique and wonderful qualities.

Isabel, Supervisor. The two of you play the game You Have It, I Want It (see page 20 in this book). Isabel has it, the Supervisor wants it.

Ghost, Isabel, Supervisor. The three of you play Two-way Conversation (see page 11 in this book). Isabel is in the middle. The Ghost and Supervisor would, of course, each choose a topic suited to his own goals or personality.

THE HEIRESS page 112

Catherine, Dr. Sloper, Morris. Imagine that you are an animal whose nature is in some way like that of the character you are portraying. Dr. Sloper, for example, could be a bear, because he is forceful and rushes straight and overpoweringly to the point. Or he might be an easily disgruntled old lion. However, the players should not consult among themselves or agree on the cast of animals before beginning the improvisation. When all have decided privately what animals they have become, play the scene from *The Heiress* in your own words and with your own movements. Remember that you are now an animal. Your own words are grunts, growls, howls, hisses, etc. Although your aim is also to give the impression of an animal's movements, you may find it a hindrance to play the scene on your hands and knees.

Morris, Dr. Sloper. Improvise a scene in which Dr. Sloper is reading a newspaper or book, when Morris enters. Morris has come to ask permission to marry Catherine. But Dr. Sloper refuses to remove his attention from his reading, to even acknowledge Morris's presence. Morris attempts to interrupt Dr. Sloper's concentration.

ANTIGONE page 116

Antigone, Haemon. In their opening speeches, the two characters refer to events which occurred the night before. Select appropriate background music, and, using free dance- or ballet-like movements, improvise a scene depicting those events. Following this, you might select new background music and improvise the current scene in dance form.

Antigone, Haemon. Play the scene in your own words while standing ten feet apart. Try to discover ways of using the distance to emphasize your feelings. You might also perform a similar improvisation, in which you play the scene in your own words while performing mundane tasks. You might be eating lunch, or one might be repairing a broken chair while the other sews. Watch, this time, for ways that you can use your body to emphasize feelings.

ANTIGONE page 120

Creon, Antigone. Imagine that Creon is a U.S. Senator who opposes amnesty for draft dodgers. Antigone, his daughter, favors amnesty and is planning to accompany a protest march to Washington. The march will be covered by T.V., radio, and the newspapers. Improvise a domestic scene between Senator Creon and Antigone.

Creon, Antigone. The two of you face each other. By turns, each gives his partner as many reasons as he can for resenting him. For examples, "You always pick on me," and "You always try to displease me." Afterwards, you might stand back to back, and by turns each tell the other how you would like him to behave. "I wish you would pay more attention to me," and "I wish you would show more respect for me," for examples.

Creon, Antigone. Act out the conflict between the two characters as a hand ballet—that is, using stylized, ballet-like movements of your hands and arms alone.

OF THEE I SING page 124

Wintergreen, Mary. Imagine that Wintergreen and Mary are sitting on a park bench. Improvising, Wintergreen begins to describe his political plans or philosophy to Mary. He might, for instance, explain to her a poll he plans to conduct. Since you (as Wintergreen) are improvising the poll as you go along, you are bound to pause occasionally. When Wintergreen does pause, Mary eagerly speaks up and supplies the next word for him. Wintergreen accepts Mary's word, as though it were exactly the one he had in mind, and continues his monologue from it. And Mary, listening intently, continues to fill in his pauses, each time trying to stay as close as she can to the general sense of the monologue. Of course, the words Mary supplies will probably not be the ones which you (as Wintergreen) would have chosen; you must remain relaxed, willing to let your monologue develop in whatever direction Mary's words might send it.

You can reverse the situation. That is, Mary improvises a monologue, and Wintergreen fills the pauses. You might imagine that the two of you are in Mary's kitchen. Mary's monologue might be a description of a special form of cooking or an explanation of why she likes to travel, for examples.

Wintergreen, Mary. Imagine that the two of you are in your seventies. Improvise a scene in which, as you sit in your living room, you reminisce about the course of your lives from the time of your first meeting.

Mary. Suppose that it is a week or so after the close of the excerpt in *Scenes for Acting and Directing Vol. 1.* Improvise a phone conversation with an imaginary female friend, in which you describe that first meeting with Wintergreen.

Wintergreen. Improvise a phone conversation similar to the one just above, but in which you describe the meeting to an imaginary male friend.

THE MAN WHO CAME TO DINNER page 128

Maggie, Whiteside. Select a small object—a book, softball, small pillow, or the like. Maggie is standing; Whiteside remains seated, as though in a wheelchair. Improvise a "conversation" without actually speaking. That is, express your attitudes, feelings, and reactions only by handling the object. The object is passed back and forth between you (like the give-and-take of a verbal conversation), each of you having your "say." Remember that, just as you would focus your attention on your partner's words in a verbal conversation, your attention must remain on the object and what is happening to it. That is the only way you will know what your partner is "saying" and, in turn, the only way you will be able to "speak" to your partner. For example, Maggie might begin the action by taking the object and holding it lovingly. In a happy state of mind, she hands it to Whiteside. Responding cynically to Maggie's happiness, Whiteside might slam the object to the floor. Maggie might pick it up, twisting it about in frustration, and place it deliberately and forcefully on Whiteside's knees. Whiteside might respond by raising it threateningly toward Maggie...and so on.

Maggie, Whiteside. Improvise a scene which could have occurred earlier on the same day as the excerpt in *Scenes for Acting and Directing Vol. 1.* Maggie tells Whiteside that she is going out for the afternoon with Bert Jefferson. Whiteside tries to dissuade her.

GENERATION page 133

Walter, Doris. Improvise a scene which could have occurred an hour or so before the opening of the excerpt in *Scenes for Acting and Directing Vol. 1.* Walter has just come home. Doris tells him that her father called unexpectedly from the airport and will be arriving soon for dinner.

Doris, Bolton. Suppose the situation in the excerpt were reversed. That is, Doris has come to Chicago to visit her father. Remember they have not seen each other since before Doris was married, and Bolton would be anxious to know how she has fared. Improvise a scene set in the office of Bolton's executive suite. Doris is attempting to describe her new life-style to her father. Bolton however, is continually interrupted by the office intercom.

Doris, Bolton, Walter. Play Two-way Conversation (described on page 11). Bolton is in the middle. The topic you choose does not necessarily have to be related to what the characters discuss in the excerpt. It could be one as seemingly insignificant as "Winter Weather." However, remember that you *are* Doris, Bolton, or Walter, and you have particular attitudes toward each of the others. If, because of your relationship with one of the other players, your conversation begins to drift into another topic, let it.

Bolton, Walter. Play the variation of the game Simultaneous Conversation (see page 10).

THE BARRETTS OF WIMPOLE STREET page 142

Barrett. Imagine that you have arrived at the Gates of Heaven. There is an angel guarding the Gates. To be admitted, you must convince the angel that you are worthy. Improvise a monologue in which you attempt to do so. (Keep in mind that you are talking to an invisible angel.)

Barrett, Reporter. Suppose that Barrett has recently been elected president of the Orphans Society, a charitable organization to which all the elite of London society belong. Improvise a scene in which a reporter has come to interview

Barrett for a magazine article. The interviewer is more interested in learning about Barrett, his personality, than about the Orphans Society.

The Barrett Children, Leader. Play the game What I Was Doing (described on page 8). However, instead of "Freeze," the leader calls "Father!" as if Barrett had just walked in on your frivolity. Then, when you invent a reason for your position, imagine that it is to Barrett that you are giving it. It will be more an excuse than a reason.

THE BARRETTS OF WIMPOLE STREET page 150

Henrietta, Policeman. Henrietta took her father's car to buy a birthday gift for Elizabeth. Though it was the only way she could get to the store, Barrett had forbidden her to use the car. Then, while hurrying home, Henrietta made a careless left turn and caused an accident between two other cars, though her car was not even touched. The policeman has now brought everyone involved, including Henrietta, to the police station. Improvise a scene between Henrietta and the policeman. The policeman wants to call Barrett at his office. Also, it is now four o'clock, and Barrett will be home by five.

Henrietta, Barrett, Elizabeth. Improvise a "courtroom drama." Imagine that Henrietta is on trial for treason, accused of attempting to pry military secrets from Captain Cook. She is now on the witness stand. Barrett is the State attorney prosecuting the case, and who is now examining Henrietta. Elizabeth is the judge.

You might similarly improvise the excerpt in *Scenes for Acting and Directing Vol. 1* as a courtroom situation. You would play the excerpt in your own words. Barrett would be the State attorney, Elizabeth the judge. Henrietta would be on the stand, accused of those "crimes" that her father accuses her of in the excerpt.

THE BARRETTS OF WIMPOLE STREET page 157

Barrett, Elizabeth. As in the excerpt in *Scenes for Acting and Directing Vol. 1,* Barrett has chosen not to see or communicate with Elizabeth for the past ten days. But he can scarcely bear the separation any longer. Improvise a scene in which the two of you now encounter each other by accident at a bus stop. There are people standing all around you. Remember that Barrett's heart would be full of the same emotions he expresses in the excerpt.

Barrett, Elizabeth. There is a great deal of tension between Barrett and Elizabeth in this excerpt. In large part, people display tension nonverbally by eye contact or avoidance, body language, facial expressions, etc. Play the scene as though you were doing it in your own words. But, instead of in words, communicate your feelings and reactions in *silence* to each other.

SCENES FOR ACTING AND DIRECTING, VOL. 2

THE DIARY OF ANNE FRANK pages 1 and 6
Anne, Peter, Extras. The two of you, Anne and Peter, stand on opposite sides of a table (a real one, not imaginary). Imagine that it is cleaning day in your one-room household, and that you are washing and drying dishes. Each of you is in love with the other. But neither of you is sure of exactly how the other feels about you. Improvise, *in silence,* a scene in which each of you attempts to express those feelings to the other. However, while you are nearly bursting with the need to communicate your intimate feelings, all around you the elders of the household (perhaps eight or ten extras) are also busily cleaning. The extras are dusting furniture, scrubbing the floor, washing walls and windows, and so on—a crowded, bustling scene. Unlike Anne and Peter, the extras are allowed to speak. Their object is to distract the lovers. They might crowd, ask questions of either of the younger people, ask them to hold objects, even require one of them to help with another job, etc.—whatever might normally occur in such a situation. As Anne or Peter, remember that you must uncomplainingly obey your elders.

Anne, Peter. Improvise a scene in which the two of you are trapped. There is no way out, and very little possibility of rescue. For example, you might have become trapped in a cave while on a hike. Or, you could accidentally have become locked in a room of a building which is to be demolished tomorrow morning.

Imagine that Peter is wanted by the police. Improvise a scene in which the two of you are hiding in a mountain cabin. There is no place left to go. And you know it is only a matter of a short time, perhaps a couple hours at most, before the authorities arrive. The two of you are preparing a meal. However, at no time during the improvisation does either of you mention the impending arrival of the police.

A MAN FOR ALL SEASONS page 9
More, Henry. Suppose that More is a farmer. Henry is a land developer who wants More's land. From those suppositions, improvise a game of You Have It, I Want It. Unlike the game as it is described on page 20, in this situation you will both know what it is that Henry wants and More has. Yet you must not refer to it by name, only as "it."

A MAN FOR ALL SEASONS page 15
Cast. Invent a scene which takes place in an airplane. Alice, Margaret, Roper, and More are playing cards, conversing, or the like. The Jailer, who is the copilot, comes back to the passenger compartment with terrible news. (The Jailer has not told the others beforehand what the news will be.) How would each character react in such a situation?

Imagine that all of you are on a picnic. The general mood is pleasant. Improvise a scene in which the mood changes drastically several times. (The changes should be caused by outside events—storms, meteors, explosions, etc.—rather than, say, by one of you picking a fight with another.) How will each express his mood change, and what will happen in your relationships with each other?

Alice, More, Roper. Invent a scene which could have taken place prior to the excerpt. The three of you debate what you should do when you visit More. The scene could be set in the More household or while you are walking to the jail in a rain storm.

THE CRUCIBLE page 22
Elizabeth, Proctor. Imagine that you, Elizabeth, want your husband to leave the house for awhile. But imagine also that you cannot tell him why. You have a secret reason for wanting him to leave, some ulterior motive which you do not want to reveal. However, Proctor has a secret motive, too. You, Proctor, do not want to leave the house at this time. Although you have a very definite reason for staying home, it is one which you do not want to reveal to your wife. Improvise a domestic scene in which each of you attempts to get your own way. It might be helpful to be involved in some sort of domestic business while developing the improvisation, such as clearing the dinner table.

THE CRUCIBLE page 28
All Eight Performers. Divide into two "hostile" groups. For example, one group might be of labor union pickets and the other of strike breakers, or one might be of left wing political demonstrators while the other is of right wingers. (You will find that this exercise will work best if you base it on a real current social conflict. But that does not mean you must take a role on the side you happen to agree with.) Then, improvise a confrontation, physically nonviolent, of course. Your object is to convince your opponents to come over to your view. At the same time, your object is to stick to your view and not to give in to your opponents, who are also trying to convince *you.*

It might be interesting to try this exercise in character, acting in the roles of the characters you portray in the excerpt in *Scenes for Acting and Directing Vol. 2.* All eight of you perform, in pantomime, some kind of communal activity. You might imagine yourselves building a house, for example.

All but Hale, Proctor, and Elizabeth leave the room. Imagine that the room is the lobby of a restaurant or hotel. Hale, Proctor, and Elizabeth are talking, paying no attention to the doorway. The rest of the players begin to enter, one by one. Each must improvise an entrance which will command the attention of those already present. (It should be a plausible entrance, not such as running in and making a loud noise or knocking someone over.) However, if the others do not feel compelled to respond and pay no attention to him, the player must go out and try again. The rest of the group, watching the improvisation, let him know if he has not succeeded by calling out, "Again" or "Go back." When everyone has succeeded in entering, the game reverses. Each player must exit. He must invent a plausible exit line which will cause the rest to notice his leaving. Again, if no one pays attention, he must return and try again. This continues until all but one player has left. For fun, the last player might invent some sort of closing flourish, a line or action.

THE POTTING SHED page 39
James, Callifer. Improvise a scene in which the two of you meet in an airport. One of you is waiting to board a plane. The other is here to meet an arrival in another part of the airport. At first you are strangers to each other. But it dawns on one, perhaps both, of you that you had been friends many years ago. Though you naturally would like to get reacquainted, each of you is under pressure of other business. One must catch his plane on time. The other must be sure not to miss the person he is here to meet.

THE POTTING SHED page 44
Sara, James. This is a situation for exploring Sara's and James' feelings and attitudes about love, marriage, and religion. Suppose that they had had a son, and that their son is now engaged to be married. Suppose, too, that his fiancee's family is of an "unusual" (i.e., not Church of England) faith—Greek Orthodox or Jewish, for examples. Improvise a conversation which takes place in a taxi as you, as Sara and James, are on your way to meet your son's future in-laws.

In the excerpt, James and Sara discuss their attitudes toward the critical human matters of life, death, love, and loss. This situation might help you to determine better the differences in the two characters' attitudes and to discover ways of expressing your particular character's attitudes. Imagine a crisis occurring in your, the Callifer's, household. About a half hour ago, James received word that your daughter has been reported missing from a church group with which she had been camping in the wilderness. Sara was out shopping when the call came. Improvise a scene in which Sara returns home, and James breaks the bad news.

SHADOW AND SUBSTANCE pages 47and 51
Brigid,Canon. Imagine that you, Brigid, are a little girl who is lost in the Great Forest. And imagine that you, Canon, are a kindly old woodsman. Improvise an encounter in which the little girl spins a woeful but fanciful tale of adventures to explain how she got into her predicament. Of course, the woodsman doubts her story. But, having a grandfatherly heart, he attempts to respond throughout with good advice. Play You Have It, I Want It (described on page 20). Each of you takes a turn in the "I want it" role.

SHADOW AND SUBSTANCE pages 56

O'Flingsley, Francis. Invent a scene in which the two of you, as O'Flingsley and Francis, are waiting outside the Canon's office. The Canon cannot be disturbed right now. Naturally, each of you believes that your business with the Canon is more important than the other's. So, each of you wants to be first to see him when he is free.

Canon, O'Flingsley. Imagine that O'Flingsley, a black, is leader of a student organization in a high school which has mostly black students. Canon is the principal of the school. He is white and an "old fashioned" scholar. He has a painful back ailment. Invent a scene in which O'Flingsley has come to the principal's office to attempt to convince the principal that black history courses should be offered in the school.

THE LARK and SAINT JOAN pages 61 and 68

Joan, her Parents. Invent a situation in which Joan tells her parents that she has decided to join a team of medical missionaries headed for some remote, primitive, unmapped region of the world. The parents attempt to dissuade her from going. Joan, not wanting to leave without her parents' blessing, must convince them of her sincere determination.

Charles, Salesman. Invent a situation in Charles's home, in which the salesman tries to talk Charles into buying a very attractive and very expensive (but that does not necessarily mean high quality) encyclopedia. Imagine that you are a high-pressure salesman, always working on the other person's weaknesses and trying to turn his own doubts and excuses against him. And how do you, as Charles, deal with such a situation?

Entire Cast. A game: Charles moves about the room, performing a variety of actions, such as opening a door, sitting on a chair, writing his name on a chalkboard—whatever occurs to him at the moment. But every time he begins an action, the other players gather round, scolding, nagging, or demanding favors from him. "You promised to wash the windows today," one might scold. Another might demand, "Get out of my chair, you lazy good-for-nothing." Someone might say, "Come on, Charles. Loan me five dollars. You owe me a favor." So it continues, the other players following Charles like noisy geese.

MARY STUART and MARY OUEEN OF SCOTLAND pages 73 and 80

Elizabeth, Mary. Suppose that Elizabeth is Mary's mother. Elizabeth, whose own marriage had been unsuccessful, strongly disapproves of her daughter's current boyfriend. But Mary, despite her mother, wants to continue seeing her boyfriend. Improvise a scene in which Mary is preparing for a date, and Elizabeth attempts to dissuade her from going out.

Mary, Elizabeth, Leicester. Imagine that the three of you are at a party in honor of Leicester, who is a well-known author. The three of you were introduced to each other just a short while ago. Each woman feels attracted to Leicester, and he, in turn, finds *both* of them attractive. Invent a scene of party conversation among the three of you, in which Mary and Elizabeth are competing for Leicester's attention, each trying to let him know that she would like to get to know him more personally. Naturally, Leicester does not want either woman to get the impression that he is favoring the other.

UNCLE VANYA page 92
Elena, Vanya. Imagine that you, Elena, are a lively, flirtatious debutante. And, Vanya, you are an old family gardener. The two of you are in a secluded garden, where Elena has come to write a letter to her special boyfriend. Improvise a scene in which Elena would like Vanya to leave, but Vanya is heedlessly bent on telling her about all the plants in his garden.

Suppose the excerpt had been set at a ball, and Elena and Vanya had been dancing instead of talking. To a recording of a Strauss waltz, improvise such a scene, a dance in which the two of you express wordlessly the same feelings as Elena and Vanya express in the excerpt.

UNCLE VANYA page 95
Elena, Sonia. Suppose that Sonia is Elena's younger sister. Sonia has come home from college. While she was away, her boyfriend, Jim, left for military service. What she does not know, however, and what Elena has been keeping secret from her, is that Jim and Elena were married before he left. Suppose, too, that today is the day of Jim's return. Improvise a scene in which the two of you, Sonia and Elena, are anxiously expecting Jim's arrival. As you reminisce about old times, you might be looking through a picture album or working in a photo lab.

CAREER pages 99 and 103
Barbara, Sam. Imagine that the two of you are walking home from school. Improvise a scene in which Sam wants very much to tell Barbara that he has decided to quit school. But Barbara is in a talkative mood and chatters without letup, breathlessly interested only in telling the latest school gossip, describing a recent movie, or the like. The improvisation is over when Sam succeeds in getting Barbara's attention long enough to tell her his decision. Then, you might reverse the situation. For instance, Barbara wants to tell Sam that her family has decided to move to another part of the country; but all that Sam is interested in talking about are his plans, for example, to hitchhike across Europe this summer.

Imagine that you are a married couple, but you have come to the joint conclusion that your three-year marriage is unsalvageably over. Improvise a scene in which the two of you are in a cafe. You sit silently, communicating your feelings without words.

The two of you are watching a tennis match. You are engaged and have just decided to get married. You sit silently, communicating your feelings wordlessly.

STREET SCENE pages 107 and 113
Shirley, Vincent. Improvise a chance meeting. When it occurs, Shirley is carrying a prayer book and is on her way to a service at a local synagogue.

Rose, Shirley. Imagine that, shortly after the events in the excerpts, Rose moved away and lost contact with the Kaplans. Several years have passed. Improvise a scene in which the two of you meet by chance in the busy bargain basement of a department store. Sam, who dropped out of law school, is a shoe clerk elsewhere in the store.

Sam, Rose. Suppose you have not seen each other since the time of the excerpts, several years ago. Improvise a scene in which you now meet by chance on a busy street corner. Neither of you is married. But, in what other ways might your respective lives have changed, if at all, since you were neighbors in the tenement? What has happened to you, who have you become over the years? You might then improvise the situation again, but supposing that each of you is married, to see how that fact might affect your reactions to each other.

THE SILVER CORD pages 117, 121 and 126
Cast. Each of these three groups plays a variation of the game Who Am I? (page 21): Robert, Mrs. Phelps, Hester; David, Mrs. Phelps, Christina; Hester, Christina, Mrs. Phelps. The third player named in the group leaves the room or retreats beyond hearing, while the other two decide on the basic situation to be improvised. They recall their partner and begin to improvise the situation. The third player, as yet ignorant of her role in the situation, attempts to adapt her responses to the action and to play into it. The improvisation is over when she is able to make it clear, by her responses to the other players, that she has discovered where she is and her specific role in the situation.

Each situation should be planned as one which is in some way negative for the third player. For example, Robert and Mrs. Phelps might decide that they are the dean and the principal of a high school, and that Hester is to be a student they want to expel because of her political activities.

Robert, David. Imagine that it is sometime prior to the events in the excerpts. You are on a golf course discussing your plans for the future.

Mrs. Phelps, her Friends. Imagine that Mrs. Phelps is having lunch with several friends at her country club. She describes what has been happening at home the last couple days.

THE SEA GULL page 130

Nina. Select an object, such as a fan, a school yearbook, a photo of a young man. Imagine that the object holds vivid memories for you. You cannot help but respond to it with strong feelings. In pantomime, improvise a series of actions which will reveal the various powerful feelings the object might provoke in you. Attempt to express a wide variety of emotions, perhaps going from sorrow to pleasure to grief to joy. You should go from state to state without breaks. Remember, too, that the transitions between emotional states must be expressed as believably as the emotions themselves. While you are improvising, you may imagine any other props you might need.

Nina, Trepleff, Doubles. Nina's double reads the script aloud. Each time her double pauses, Nina supplies the unspoken thoughts implied by the pause, as though she were her own inner voice. Trepleff performs a similar improvisation with his double.

THE FOURPOSTER page 135

He, She. Imagine that the two of you have been married only a couple years at this time. You are in your first house. HIS boss is to arrive at any moment for dinner. HE is nervous and apprehensive, wants to make a good impression. SHE is attempting to put the last touches to the table and finish the cooking. But SHE is distracted. SHE is more concerned about your year-old son in the next room, who is fretful because he is teething. Preparations for the dinner party are rather disorganized and running late. Improvise a scene of domestic chaos in which HE frantically and clumsily attempts to "help out." Your scene will be an interplay of HER distraction and HIS anxiety.

Imagine that you are at an amusement park. Improvise a variety of activities, such as riding the merry-go-round, eating taffy and cotton candy, arguing about what to do next, looking at yourselves in distorted mirrors, etc. Keep up a fairly steady flow of conversation. However, speak only in gibberish, in nonsense language.

ANDROCLES AND THE LION page 143

Androcles,Megaera. Invent imaginary clown costumes for yourselves which depict Androcles and Megaera in exaggerated forms, with exaggerated characteristics which in some way reflect the personality of each. When you have discussed and settled on your "costumes," improvise a circus act in which you play tricks on each other. Sometimes Androcles will have the upper hand. At other times, Megaera's tricks will prevail. Use a great deal of random movement and gymnastics.

WAITING FOR LEFTY page 149

Barnes, Benjamin. Play the game Who Am I? (page 21), with Barnes as the leader. On this occasion, the game will probably work best if the situation you invent is an occupational one, as in the excerpt, rather than, say, a domestic or recreational one.

You, Benjamin, are a black. You have come to be interviewed for a teaching job in a small town which has no black residents. You did not reveal in your letter of application that you are black. Barnes is the interviewer.

You are both Chicanos. Barnes, however, for reasons of his own, is passing as an Anglo. Barnes is a high school teacher and Benjamin a student. Improvise a scene in which Benjamin approaches Barnes to ask his support in agitating for bilingual studies in the school.

INHERIT THE WIND page 154

Gallery and Jurors, Leader. In a crowd scene, each actor must create a believable character, an individual whose responses to the situation appear to be his own spontaneous ones. At the same time, the actors as a group must create the sense of a crowd's unity of purpose. Here are some games which might help establish that necessary feeling of ensemble.

The players walk randomly about the room. At an unplanned moment, the leader calls out an emotionally loaded word or phrase derived from the script. The players freeze, each expressing some kind of facial or otherwise physical reaction to the word. Possible words are Bible, Darwin, Apostles of Science, science, sin, and agnostic. After a count of five, the players continue their walks, until the leader calls another word, and so on.

In another game, the group divides into Drummondites and Bradyites and play tug of war with an imaginary rope. In effect, the group must work together for an appearance of conflict.

As a third game, the leader calls out a situation which the players then improvise, such as "happy passengers aboard a luxury liner." When the group has established that situation, the leader calls a new one, such as "the ship has been struck by an iceberg," and the players respond appropriately. Continue through several more mood changes. You can also play the game without a designated leader, with *any* player calling out a new situation.

Drummond, Brady. Improvise a scene which could have taken place on the evening before the trial. There is only one unoccupied table in the hotel dining room. You both arrive at the same time and must share it.

A game: Brady sits at a table with a book before him. If it is a red book, for example, you, as Brady, are positive that it is green. And, as Drummond, you must convince Brady that he is color blind.

SCENES FOR ACTING AND DIRECTING, VOL. 3

CYRANO DE BERGERAC page 1
Cyrano, De Guiche. Cyrano's attempts to delay de Guiche amount to a version of the game Changes (page 19, this book), To get a better feeling of this aspect of the excerpt, play a game of "instant" Changes. It might take you a couple tries to get the knack of this technique, but it can be very rewarding. It is a speeded up version of Changes, in which *each* verbal expression, movement, or gesture must cause an immediate change of character or situation. You do not take time to develop the situation. You establish it with one stroke, transform it into a new one with the next, and so on, without pause.

Before starting, make up a list of imaginary encounters which in some way reflect the relationship between Cyrano and de Guiche. The encounters you list may be as exotic, as far out, as you wish—flamboyant buccaneer and dimwitted monk, Shakespearean actor and clumsy dancer, glib salesman and slow custodian, flitting canary and glowering bulldog, for examples. Your improvisations will be from that list (though, of course, as in all improvisation, an entirely unexpected situation might sometimes crop up). You need not improvise the situations in any special order. Nor is there a rule about who must initiate a situation. There are no "turns." Either of you may change a situation at any time.

Pretend the two of you are on a basketball court. De Guiche wants to go home. Cyrano wants to "shoot a few" yet. But de Guiche is responsible for checking the ball into the equipment room. Improvise a scene in which Cyrano dribbles, weaves, engages de Guiche in a rapid-fire passing routine, etc., while inventing reasons to convince de Guiche not to leave. The improvisation is over when one of you wins his wish.

The two of you meet in a restaurant or waiting room of some kind many years after the evening on which the excerpt takes place. No longer adversaries, you reminisce about that evening.

CYRANO DE BERGERAC page 9
Cyrano, Roxane. In the excerpt, much of the communication between the two characters takes place under their words, as long-time understandings do. For a better understanding of the relationship between Cyrano and Roxane, try this exercise. Sit on the floor, back to back, eyes closed. Now, communicate in silence, simply by the ways in which your backs touch. The communication should include a greeting, some exchange of feelings or ideas, and a farewell.

ANNE OF THE THOUSAND DAYS pages 19 and 24
Anne, Henry. Imagine that Anne is a seven-year-old child. Henry is a young

motorcycle police officer. Anne is on a playground playing with her favorite toy. Along comes Henry, who attempts to convince her to join the other children on the playground equipment. Then, reverse roles. Henry is the child. Anne, his nurse, would like him to play with the other children on the swings and slides.

Improvise a "split-screen" scene in which a young wife and her soldier husband are each writing a letter to the other. Sitting at her desk, the wife verbalizes the lines as she writes them. When she pauses at the end of a thought, the husband immediately takes up the narrative in the same manner, speaking the lines as he writes them. Thus, the "letter" continues, back and forth, each player picking it up whenever the other pauses. In effect, you will be improvising a narrative which will reveal your thoughts and feelings about the course of your relationship. For example, you might begin by remembering the time you moved into your first home together and see what develops from there.

Develop a conversation in which the only words you use are each other's names. Anne may say only "My Lord." Henry may say only "Nan." Begin by looking into each other's eyes. After a sense of contact has been established, you should be able to communicate a variety of messages through the tone, pitch, and inflections of your voice.

ARMS AND THE MAN page 31
Raina, Bluntschli. Suppose that you were once in love with each other. But it developed that each had habits or attitudes which continually got on the other's nerves, and neither of you was willing to change his or her own ways. Consequently, your relationship broke up. Imagine that now, after a year's separation, you have agreed to meet again in an amusement park. Improvise that meeting. You discover that you are still in love. You discover the same old nagging habits and the same unwillingness to change. Each of you believes the rendezvous was the other's idea.

ARMS AND THE MAN page 37
Sergius, Bluntschli. Imagine that you are football players from rival schools. You meet on Raina's front porch. Each of you bears a corsage and believes he has a date with Raina. The improvisation is over when one of you persuades the other to retreat.

Bluntschii, Sergius, Raina. Imagine yourselves on a picnic. Bluntschli and Sergius both want to be alone with Raina. So, each attempts to devise ways of getting rid of the other. (Raina must not remain passive, but must create ways of participating in the action.)

SQUARING THE CIRCLE pages 43 and 47
Cast, Abram. The four of you are two married couples (Tonya and Abram, Vasya

and Ludmilla). Imagine that you are in a TV studio. There are two sets: half of the studio represents one couple's apartment; the other half represents the other couple's. There are two cameras, one focused on each couple on their respective set.

Both couples improvise upon the same idea. That is, each lives in a small, crowded apartment. In each case, some in-laws have just left after a long and unexpected visit. The marrieds are now straightening the furniture and having a lively discussion about the visit. However, one couple is greatly *amused* about the visit, while on the other set the second couple is greatly *annoyed.*

The couples improvise alternately. One couple starts the action, while the other two players assume frozen postures which suggest they are engaged in a conversation. When the first couple comes to a natural pause, the second couple (as though the director had thrown the switch which changes cameras) begins to improvise, picking up on a word or idea used by the first players. The first players fall silent now that they are off camera, though they need not freeze. Then, when the second couple comes to a pause, the first takes over again-and so on, the scene switching back and forth as though a director were switching the master camera control. Remember that time does not stand still while you are off camera. You cannot simply take up where you left off a few minutes ago. Each time the scene switches, time has moved forward. For variety, you might try the improvisation with one partner of each couple delighted and the other annoyed by the visit, so the two couples are evenly balanced.

Vasya, Ludmilla. Improvise the following scenes, in which each of you expresses her or his thoughts and feelings using a one-word vocabulary. Vasya can say only "Ludmilla." Ludmilla can say only "Vasya."

1. You are in a small car or on a motorcycle on your way to an important meeting. You develop motor trouble. As the evening grows chillier, Vasya tries to fix the motor. Before leaving home, Ludmilla had pleaded for Vasya to inspect the motor.
2. You have been married a couple months. Ludmilla has not yet been able to serve Vasya a meal he likes. As Vasya enters now, Ludmilla proceeds to serve him a lavish six-course Chinese dinner. But he cannot eat it. He hates Chinese food, cannot manipulate chopsticks, and breaks out in an allergic rash from the cooking fumes.
3. Vasya, an amateur naturalist, has persuaded Ludmilla to accompany him on a butterfly hunt. The hunt finds the two of you in a swamp on an intolerably hot, sticky afternoon.

MAN AND SUPERMAN page 52

Tanner, Ann. Suppose Tanner is a brilliant research scientist. Ann is his brilliant and very attractive assistant. As the two of you have worked side by side over the past year, Tanner has become emotionally dependent on Ann.

But he hides his feelings behind a mask of indifference, because he is unsure of himself. He is uncertain whether he has fallen in love with Ann because of her bright mind or because of her physical appearance. During the same time, Ann has come to love Tanner as well. But she, too, is under tension. On one hand, another man has been paying her lavish attention. On the other, there is Tanner's enigmatic indifference.

Improvise a scene in which the two of you are working in your cluttered laboratory. You are nearing what you think will be a breakthrough in your experiments. Ann, distracted by her personal conflict, knocks over and breaks some important equipment. She tells Tanner it would be best if she were to resign. Tanner will not (or cannot) let her go.

THE SCHOOL FOR SCANDAL page 57

Sir Peter, Lady Teazle. For an idea of mid-seventeenth century life-styles, you might find it worthwhile to study the period in an art history book. Portraits as well as paintings and etchings of everyday life will give you an idea of the dress and mannerisms of the time. And of course an art museum is always a good source of ideas.

Having done that, improvise in pantomime a series of tableaux which "illustrate" this excerpt from *The School for Scandal.* Concentrate on capturing the feeling of the period by using the mannerisms and postures yet discovered in your research. Let your tableaux evolve one after the other. Do not pause to "set them up."

BLITHE SPIRIT page 61

Charles, Ruth, Eivira. Play a game of Two-way Conversation (page 11). Naturally, Charles is in the middle. The women should attempt to select topics which in some way are appropriate to their characters in the excerpt.

The excerpt takes place in a living room, a setting with which the characters would be intimately familiar. When you play the excerpt, it is important that you give that impression of domestic familiarity. Here is an exercise which might help. Arrange a number of simple props to create the impression of a living room—chairs, a table, perhaps another table to represent a piano, etc. Walk through the "set" to get the feel of the arrangement. Then, *blindfolded,* improvise a domestic scene in which each of you uses every prop at least once. For example, Elvira might serve (using necessary props) refreshments to Ruth and Charles, her guests. Attempt to behave normally, as though you were not blindfolded. Thus, bumping into any of the props cannot be explained in terms of your blindness. Rather, you must justify the contact, as though you had intended it.

JUNO AND THE PAYCOCK pages 69 and 72

Jerry, Mary. Create a scene in which you, Jerry, attempt to persuade Mary to go to a baseball game with you this afternoon. But Mary resists. As Mary, you do not want to tell Jerry that you are expecting a phone call from an old boyfriend this afternoon. The improvisation is over when Mary must admit the reason for her reluctance.

Mary. Suppose that years have passed since the events of the excerpts. You have a child now, a little girl. The two of you live in a tenement in Dublin. Your daughter has just found a copy of the poem, which appears at the end of the second excerpt, and is curious about it. Improvise a monologue in which you explain to her the meaning of the poem to you. At the same time, you of course are revealing your feelings about that time in your life and what has happened to you since.

GIRLS IN UNIFORM pages 75 and 80

2 Bernburgs, 2 Manuelas. This improvisation can help you bring out and better understand the feelings and unspoken thoughts which motivate the characters in the excerpt. You will have to have read the excerpt and have a good idea of how the action develops.

Two players, both at once, take the part of Manuela. One is the outer, the "real," Manuela. The other is her inner self or voice, who sticks with the "real" Manuela as closely as a shadow. In the same way, two players take the part of Bernburg. Under those conditions, the four of you improvise the meeting which occurs in the excerpt (i.e., improvise the idea, the sense of what happens in the excerpt rather than playing it line for line). As the *outer* Bernburg and Manuela improvise the scene, the inner Bernburg and Manuela give voice to the unspoken thoughts and feelings of the "real" players. For example, at times Manuela's inner voice might behave like a guardian angel, approving Manuela's actions. At other times, the inner voice might behave like a devil, urging Manuela to act against her own best judgement. At all times, the inner voice expresses the fears and yearnings which Manuela feels but does not express directly. Bernburg's inner voice does the same for her. When you have worked through the improvisation, the "real" players exchange roles with their inner voices.

You should try to improvise this situation as you would any other scene involving four players. Try to avoid speaking over each other's lines. This might be difficult at first, since no one can know who will speak next. But with some practice the four of you should be able to share the scene equally, each listening and responding at the appropriate time.

2 Heads, 2 Bernbergs. Improvise the scene between Head and Bernburg in the same manner as above.

THE MOON IS DOWN page 85

Molly, Tonder. Improvise a game of Who Am I? (page 21). Each of you takes a turn as lead player.

Devise a scene in which Molly, driving a lonely highway, gives a lift to a handsome young hitchhiker (Tonder, naturally). As the two of you are riding along, each finds that she or he is attracted to the other. However, Molly must also discover something which terrifies her about the young man. Tonder must play into Molly's improvisation.

Molly, imagine that you are the daughter of a socially prominent and perhaps rather snobbish family. Tonder, you are self-educated and have a modest job. Also, your parents were Chinese immigrants. The two of you have been seeing each other steadily for a month. But Molly's father has now discovered your relationship. From those suppositions, invent a scene in which Molly tells Tonder that she must break with him. It is a moonlit night. You have just come from a movie. You are on Molly's porch.

R.U.R. pages 90 and 96

Consider that the robots were *invented,* not born. While in many respects the robots are very similar to humans, still they are a different order of beings. In portraying a robot in *R.U.R.,* your problem is to project that balance of "humanness" and "robotness"; if too much of either, then the terror of the situation is lost.

Cast. You will need two soundtracks for this exercise. The first should be a recording of a work by Edgar Varese, John Cage, or an electronic composer such as Morton Subotnick. Parts of the soundtrack of the movie 2001 might work well. The other soundtrack should be of a work by a composer such as Prokofiev, Tchaikovsky, or Brahms-music in a more "romantic" vein than that of the first soundtrack.

Divide into two groups, robots and humans. The robots listen to the first soundtrack. Each lets himself go with the music and begins to improvise movements in accompaniment with it, individually and with other robots, whatever develops at the moment. The humans do the same to the "romantic" music. The two groups may improvise alternately, but you might find it worthwhile for both to work at once, each player concentrating on his own "robotness" or "humanness" despite the presence of the other soundtrack. After improvising in that manner for awhile, reverse the situation, robots improvising to the second soundtrack, humans to the first. Afterwards, you might want to discuss the experiences.

Robots, Leader. The rest of the group might also like to take part in this interesting exercise. It would probably be helpful if the leader were someone who has had experience with this sort of improvisation. The leader and the players must cooperate to create the following situation. The leader must be gentle and persuasive. Each player must give himself wholly to the leader's suggestions.

Lie quietly and comfortably on the floor, eyes closed, your entire body relaxed. Try not to think of anything. After a few moments, the leader gently asks you to awaken. As you wake, you discover that you are someone else. You have your own body. But, inside, you are a brand new person. You have no memory of how this happened. The leader suggests that you stand up and tells you that you are in a familiar place. He might tell you that you are in your home, a playground, factory, or hospital, etc. Move about as he describes some of the place to you. Through your new senses, respond to and get to know this "familiar" place you have never seen before and the other people you encounter in it. After awhile, the leader asks you to return to your original position. Relax, close your eyes. After another few moments, the leader asks you to awaken to yourself again.

Primus, Helena Glory. The two of you have not met before. Imagine that you have arrived at a restaurant at the same time. There is but one table left. Improvise a scene in which you decide who will take the table or, perhaps, decide to take it together. At some point, Helena must discover that Primus is a robot. But, Primus must not explicitly reveal it to her.

You might improvise similar meetings, in different settings, with any of the several possible robot-human combinations. It might also be interesting to improvise the same sort of first meeting between Primus and the robot Helena.

THE DOCTOR IN SPITE OF HIMSELF pages 100 and 103

It would be a good idea to do some research on *commedia dell' arte,* the type of comedy from which the style of Moliere's play was derived. Characteristic *of commedia dell' arte* was a broad, open, almost slapstick style. The plot was loose, often improvised from outline. The characters were stereotypes. The actors often wore masks to identify the characters. The following exercises might help you get into the *commedia dell' arte* feeling of these excerpts.

Martine, Sganarelle. To background music from the film *Tom Jones,* or to similar music, improvise a sequence of actions which tells the story of your basic relationship. This will be like a dance, your movements developing with the music.

Study the masks used in *commedia dell' arte* and pictures of typical *commedia dell' arte* characters. Then, in *commedia dell' arte* style, using authentic or homemade masks, improvise a scene in which Sganarelle returns home after his adventure in Geronte's house and tells Martine all about it. Martine is preparing dinner when he returns. Remember that, unknown to Sganarelle, Martine had initiated the adventure as a punishment for him.

Sganarelle, Geronte. Each of you takes on a greatly exaggerated personal debility—such as a nervous twitch, bobbing of the head, vibrating chin, trembling hands, or stutter—which you will sustain throughout the improvisation. Imagine, then, that you are in an antique shop. Sganarelle is the crafty, fast-talking owner. Geronte is a gullible customer who comes seeking authentic antiques for his family.

PURLIE VICTORIOUS pages 108 and 114

Cast. To help set the persuasive, rhythmical mood which recurs regularly through the excerpts, you might warm up to a recording of thd Staple Singers or another group with a similar style. Let yourself go, dancing, weaving, generally moving with the music.

In a similar vein, you might listen to a recording of the musical *Purlie.* Then, in recitative form, Purlie intones some of his longer speeches in a free-form style, and the others respond like a chorus.

Purlie, Lutlebelle. Improvise a scene in which Lutiebelle has prepared a meal which she thinks will delight Purlie. But, actually, it is exactly the sort of food he detests. Purlie must attempt to keep his distaste concealed.

Cast, Tourist. You might prefer to have only a couple members of the cast perform this at a time. Agree on the layout and furnishings of the Judson house, using some simple props to represent them if you wish. Then, invent a scene in which the white tourist stops at the house to ask for a drink of water, directions, or the like. Your aim is to establish the sense, without ever explicitly stating it, that this is the "sharecropper's farmhouse in Southern Georgia" where the excerpts are set. That is, if an observer did not already know the setting, he would get a good idea of it from the way you use and otherwise relate to the imaginary props.

TOYS IN THE ATTIC page 123

Lily, Albertine. Create a scene of mother-daughter conflict. The daughter is going to a party tonight. So, she went shopping this morning for a new dress. It was the first time she had done so without her mother going along to help. In fact, she had not told her mother she was going. The daughter now returns home with the dress she has chosen. But her mother does not approve of the dress and wants her to return it at once.

Again, imagine that the two of you are a widowed mother and her daughter. The two of you are in one room, while, unknown to the daughter, the mother's lover is in the adjoining room. The daughter has a reason for wanting to go into the other room. The mother wants to prevent her from going in.

GIGI pages 130 and 137

Alicia, Gigi. Study pictures of a variety of animals. Or, better, observe various animals firsthand at a zoo. Observe the "character" of each kind of animal, its way of moving, the distinctive aspects of its face, body, legs, wings, voice, etc. Afterwards, from memory, select one animal which in some way reminds you of the character you are portraying, of Alicia or Gigi. Imagine that you are that animal. Spend awhile moving about the acting area, getting used to your new body and voice.

Each of you is now a particular animal. Improvise a scene which takes place in a library. Alicia is the librarian. Gigi attempts to acquire an "adult" book which is kept behind the desk. Though of course you will have to use human language, try to do so in your animal voice.

Gigi, Gaston. Imagine that the two of you have been for a moonlight drive in Gaston's open sports car. Now you are parked on the shore of a placid lake. The air is mild. The moon is reflected across the water. Soft music comes from the radio. Gaston would like to kiss Gigi, and, indeed, Gigi would not be unwilling. The problem is that Gaston notices that there is a piece of Spinach stuck on Gigi's front teeth. Though he very much wants to kiss her, Gaston must not tell Gigi about her appearance.

Gaston is on the board of directors of an oil company. For the sake of experience, he is working as a mechanic at a service station. Gigi's car has not been running well. The two of you meet when she brings her car to the station to be inspected. You find yourselves attracted to each other. But each of you also has a concealed conflict. Gigi must not reveal that she has been trained not to associate with menial workers. Gaston must not reveal his true identity.

A MONTH IN THE COUNTRY pages 141 and 148

2 Veras, 2 Natallas. Improvise the plot outline of the first excerpt, using the inner-outer technique suggested for *Girls in Uniform* (page 106).

Vera, Natalia. Imagine that you are sisters, about equal in age. Improvise a scene in which the two of you are shopping in a fashionable dress store. Each of you is seeking an especially alluring dress for a party next week. But, at the same time, each of you has another goal, a secret one: you do not want your sister to be more attractive than you are.

Bellaev, Vera. Improvise a scene in which Beliaev, a travel agent, is helping Vera plan a European tour. The tour is a gift from her parents. Her parents have informed Beliaev that Vera has a terminal disease and have charged him with concealing that knowledge from her, for Vera is unaware of her illness. Vera insists upon traveling alone. Beliaev cannot tell her why she must not.

Imagine that the two of you have been going steady for several years. Improvise a scene in which Beliaev returns after a year away at college. He has come to return a stack of Vera's letters, Vera does not yet know that, during their separation, Beliaev married another girl.

LADY WINDERMERE'S FAN page 153

Lady Windermere, Mrs. Erlynne. Lady Windermere is a student. Mrs. Erlynne is one of her teachers and a friend of her mother. It is sometime after class. Mrs. Erlynne is wondering what to do about Lady Windermere's latest paper. Just like the young woman's last paper and the one before that, every word is plagiarized. Just as she decides and begins to tear up the paper, Lady Windermere enters, returning for a book she had left on her seat. Lady Windermere is rather spoiled and arrogant, and her mother is a member of the board of education.

Lady Windermere, Mrs. Erlynne, Male. Improvise a scene in which a young man and his former girl friend (Mrs. Erlynne) are in a restaurant booth (or the school cafeteria or similar meeting place). They are planning a surprise party for his present girl friend. As they are whispering together, the present girl friend (Lady Windermere) comes in and discovers them. Of course they stop whispering when they see her.

NIGHT MUST FALL pages 160
Dan, Olivia. Improvise the story line of each excerpt with the following alterations. First, Dan is eight or nine years old, and Olivia is in her forties. Then, reverse the situation: Olivia is a child, Dan is middle aged.

Improvise a kind of ballet in which Dan is a flame and Olivia a moth attracted to the light. Then, reverse the situation: Dan is the moth, Olivia the flame.

Imagine that Olivia is blind. She has just gotten off a bus and is waiting for a male relative, whom she has never met, to escort her to her destination. Dan appears and offers his assistance. He is not the planned escort.

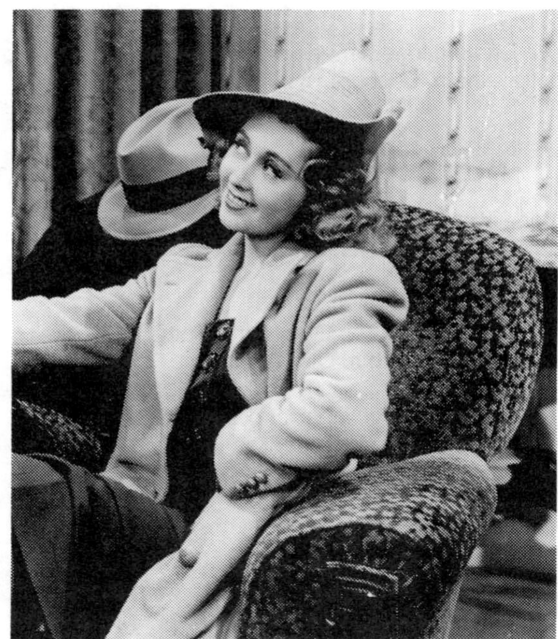

Courtesy of the William-Alan Landes Collection. Joan Blondell in one of her famous poses. Ms. Blondell stars with Frank McHugh and Sam Levene in Mervyn LeRoy's film version of John Cecil Holm's play *THREE MEN ON A HORSE*.

THREE MEN ON A HORSE, a film version of John Cecil Holm's play. What a gang of comedians. See if you can name the players. Don't miss the famous bar tender. Courtesy of Warner Brothers Pictures.

4

Scenes for Practice

In this section of the handbook, you will develop and show your understanding of the material you have learned. In Section 3 you prepared basic improvisations for scenes in my previous three scene books; I also included, in this last section, additional scenes followed by their respective improvisations. Utilizing those improvisation and the directing notes in these scenes, you can prepare your improvisations to create the necessary environment as well as develop characterizations for the plots and settings presented here.

By this time you should be fully aware of the techniques we have explored. You are looking for character motivations that are not readily available. You want to find the playwright's purpose for your character to enter and react at the precise moment, or the way the setting influences the character's actions. As a director you are also interested in determining the relations and interactions between your characters.

In Sections 2 and 3, we explored these techniques. Now it is time to use them for yourself.

In addition to the improvisations I have created, take a look at the scenes in this section and create your own improvisations to explore your characterizations.

Remember, there is no singular answer and each individual will approach the character differently. The only rule you try to apply is that an *improvised action must happen in a definite place.*

Once you have worked with this section, or if you have problems working with scenes from any of the Scenes for Acting and Directing volumes, then work these scenes again. They will be a cornerstone for you to build and rebuild characterizations.

Not all improvisations will work. Some will drift away from your goals and others will just go nowhere. Improvisations will all give you new insight into your character and the more insight you have, the better you will be at becoming the character. You will, as said in Section 2, develop the needed skills to become your own best, not worst critic, distinguishing the successful improvisations and learning from your less successful ones, while also developing the skills to solve the problems and correct your approach. Essentially, this is the section where you put form to your improvisations and develop a beginning, a middle and an end without trying to pad or fill the space. You will now improve your skills at resolving the problem and ending improvisations.

from

NIGHT MUST FALL

ACT 3, Scene 2

Emlyn Williams

It is a night in late October. The setting is the living room of Mrs. Bramson's house in a forest in the county of Essex, England. The room is lighted by a single paraffin lamp. There is a doorway leading to the sun room. (See page 160 for further background.)

As the play develops, the playwright leads the audience to expect Mrs. Bramson's murder. As a result, the audience's interest is focused not as much on the development of a murder scheme as on the characters of Dan and Olivia. The relationship between these two characters is culminated in this scene.

The servants and Mrs. Bramson's neice, Olivia, had gone for the night. Taking advantage of this situation, the young man known only as Dan has killed Mrs. Bramson, his employer, leaving her body in the sun room. He has taken the key which the old woman wore around her neck, has opened and emptied Mrs. Bramson's safe. When this scene opens, Dan, while preparing to set the house afire, has heard a sound in the sun room. He is now standing near the doorway, a chair raised over his head, ready to strike the intruder.

(*The stagger of footsteps;* **OLIVIA** *stands in the doorway to the sun-room. She has been running through the forest; her clothes are wild, her hair has fallen about her shoulders, and she is no longer wearing spectacles. She looks nearly beautiful. Her manner is quiet, almost dazed.* **DAN** *lowers the chair slowly and sits on the other side of the table. A pause.*)

OLIVIA. I've never seen a dead body before . . . I climbed through the window and nearly fell over it. Like a sack of potatoes or something. I thought it was, at first. . . . And that's murder. (*As he looks up at her.*) But it's so ordinary . . . I came back . . . (*As he lights his cigarette.*) . . . expecting . . . ha (*Laughing hysterically.*) . . . I don't know . . . and here I find you, smoking a cigarette . . . you might have been tidying the room for the night. It's so . . . ordinary. . . . (*After a pause, with a cry.*) Why don't you *say* something!

DAN. I thought you were goin' to stay the night at that feller's.

OLIVIA. I was.

DAN. What d'you come back for?

OLIVIA (*the words pouring out*). To find you out. You've kept me guessing for a fortnight. Guessing hard. I very nearly knew, all the time. But not quite. And now I do know.

DAN. Why was you so keen on finding me out?

OLIVIA (*vehemently, coming to the table*). In the same way any sane, decent-minded human would want—would want to have you arrested for the monster you are!

DAN (*quietly*). What d'you come back for?

OLIVIA. I . . . I've told you. . . .[1] (*He smiles at her slowly and shakes his head. She sits at the table and closes her eyes.*) I got as far as the edge of the wood. I could see the lights in the village . . . I came back. (*She buries her head in her arms.* **DAN** *rises, looks at her a moment regretfully, puts away his cigarette, and stands with both hands over the invalid chair.*)[2]

DAN (*casually*). She didn't keep any money anywhere else, did she?

OLIVIA. I've read a lot about evil——(**DAN** *realises his hands are wet with paraffin and wipes them on his trousers.*)

DAN. Clumsy. . . .

OLIVIA. I never expected to come across it in real life.

DAN (*lightly*). You didn't ought to read so much. I never got through a book yet. . . . But I'll read you all right. . . . (*Crossing to her, leaning over the table, and smiling at her intently.*) You haven't had a drop of drink, and

1. Both characters lie about their own motives and/or feelings. What are the true attitudes which guide each? Patterns of speech, action, posture, facial expressions, etc. should be developed to help convey a sense of these inner conflicts. The ultimate unmaskings should not be wholly unexpected.

2. Notice that when one character weakens, the other becomes stronger. Determine who is dominant at specific points. When and how is control of the scene exchanged? The wheel chair is Mrs. Bramson's.

yet you feel as if you had. You never knew there was such a secret part inside of you. All that book-learnin' and moral-me-eye here and social-me-eye there—you took that off on the edge of the wood same as if it was an overcoat . . . and you left it there!

OLIVIA. I hate you. I . . . hate you!

DAN (*urgently*).[3] And same as anybody out for the first time without their overcoat, you feel as light as air! Same as I feel, sometimes—only I never had no overcoat——(*Excited.*) Why—this is my big chance! You're the one I can tell about meself! Oh, I'm sick o' hearin' how clever everybody else is—I want to tell 'em how clever *I* am for a change! . . . Money I'm going to have, and people doin' what they're told, and *me* tellin' them to do it! There was a 'oman at the Tallboys,[4] wasn't there? She wouldn't be told, would she? She thought she was up 'gainst a soft fellow in a uniform, didn't she? She never knew it was *me* she was dealin' with—(*Striking his chest in a paroxysm of elation.*)—*Me!* And this old girl treatin' me like a son 'cause I made her think she was a chronic invalid—ha! She's been more use to me tonight (*Tapping the notes in his jacket pocket, smartly.*) than she has to any other body all her life.[5] Stupid, that's what people are . . . stupid. If those two hadn't been stupid they might be breathin' now; you're not stupid; that's why I'm talkin' to you. (*With exaggerated self-possession.*) You said just now murder's ordinary. . . . Well it isn't ordinary at all, see? And I'm not an ordinary chap. There's one big difference 'tween me and other fellows that try this game. I'll *never be found out.* 'Cause I don't care a——(*Snapping his fingers, grandly.*) The world's goin' to hear from me. That's me. (*Chuckling.*) You wait. . . . (*After a pause.*) But you can't wait, can you?

OLIVIA. What do you mean?

DAN. Well, when I say I'll never be found out, what I mean is, no living soul will be able to tell any other living soul about me. (*Beginning to roll up a sleeve, nonchalantly.*) Can you think of anybody . . . who can go tomorrow . . . and tell the police the fire at Forest

3. Study the scene closely for pattern of tempo. When and why does the tempo change?

4. A hotel. Dan refers to a woman he killed while he was employed there.

5. He refers to Mrs. Bramson.

6. Mrs. Bramson's house.

Corner[6] . . . wasn't an accident at all?

OLIVIA. I—I can.

DAN. Oh no, you can't.

OLIVIA. Why can't I?

DAN. Well, I'm up against a very serious problem, I am. But the answer to it is as simple as pie, to a fellow like me, simple as pie. . . . (*Rolling up the other sleeve a little way.*) She isn't going to be the only one . . . found tomorrow . . . in the fire at Forest Corner. . . . (*After a pause.*) Aren't you frightened? You ought to be! (*Smiling.*) Don't you think I'll do it?

OLIVIA. I know you will. I just can't realise it.

DAN. You know, when I told you all that about meself just now, I'd made up my mind then about you. (*Moving slowly after her, round the table, as she steps back towards the window.*) That's what I am, see? I make up me mind to do a thing, and I do it. . . . You remember that first day when I come in here? I said to meself then, There's a girl that's got her wits about her; she knows a thing or two; different from the others. I was right, wasn't I? You——(*Stopping abruptly, and looking round the room.*) What's that light in here?

OLIVIA. What light?

DAN. There's somebody in this room's holdin' a flashlight.

OLIVIA. It can't be in this room. . . . It must be a light in the wood.

DAN. It can't be. (*A flashlight crosses the window-curtain.* **OLIVIA** *turns and stares at it.*)

OLIVIA. Somebody's watching the bungalow. . . . (*He looks at her, as if he did not understand.*)

DAN (*fiercely*). Nobody's watching! . . . (*He runs to the window. She backs into the corner of the room.*) I'm the one that watches! They've got no call to watch me! I'll go out and tell them that, an' all! (*Opening the curtains in a frenzy.*) I'm the one that watches! (*The light crosses the window again. He stares, then claps his hands over his eyes. Backing to the sofa.*) Behind them trees, (*Clutching the invalid chair.*) Hundreds back of each tree. . . . Thousands of eyes. The whole damn world's on my track! . . . (*Sitting on the edge of the sofa,* *and listening.*) What's that? . . , Like a big wall fallin' over into the sea. . . . (*Closing his hands over his ears convulsively.*)

OLIVIA (*coming down to him*). They mustn't come in. . . .

DAN (*turning to her*). Yes, but . . . (*Staring.*) You're looking' at me as if you never seen *me* before. . . .

OLIVIA. I never have. Nobody has. You've stopped acting at last. You're real. Frightened. Like a child. (*Putting her arm about his shoulders.*) They mustn't come in. . . .

DAN. But everything's slippin' away. From underneath our feet. . . . Can't you feel it? Starting slow . . . and then hundreds of miles an hour. . . . I'm goin' backwards! . . . And there's a wind in my ears, terrible blowin' wind. . . . Everything's going past me like the telegraph-poles. . . . All the things I've never seen . . . faster and faster . . . backwards—back to the day I was born. (*Shrieking.*) I can see it coming . . . the day I was born! . . . (*Turning to her, simply.*) I'm goin' to die. (*A pause. A knock at the front door.*) It's getting cold. (*Another knock; louder. She presses his head to her.*)

OLIVIA. It's all right. You won't die. I'll tell them I *made* you do it. I'll tell lies—I'll tell——(*A third and louder knock at the front door.*)

Improvisation

NIGHT MUST FALL

Dan, Olivia. (Use the suggested improvisation on page 111.)

from

J.B.

Scene 8

Archibald MacLeish

It is a night in the present. The scene is set in a huge circus tent. In its original form, the play calls for an acting area of three levels. There is a rough side show stage. Below that is a larger area with a decrepit table and chair. Above and to one side of the stage is a platform, six feet high, with a ladder leading up to it, and with a chair. In this scene, the lower area and the platform are used and may be represented as space allows.

J. B. is a modern Job. Despite the fact that his children have died and he has lost all his money, J. B. continues to accept without question God's wise will. For Sarah, his wife, the situation is more trying. She does not have J. B.'s patience in suffering. She grows bitter from the pains of her losses.

Besides J. B. and Sarah, there are four women and a young girl (Jolly Adams) appearing in the scene. The appearance of these extra characters emphasizes the isolation of suffering. The women, through J. B. and Sarah, see and superficially discuss suffering, but only the sufferer *knows*.

A man named Nickles also appears in the scene. He is a sort of commentator akin to the chorus of classical Greek drama. Actually, Nickles is a rather broken-down actor, who, earlier in the play, had agreed to play the part of Satan. Thus, his part is a self-conscious one; the actor taking his role must remember that Nickles is an actor who is playing the role of Satan, that he is a character playing another character. The scene's final line suggests Nickle's true attitude toward J. B.'s situation.

(There is no light but the glow on the canvas sky, which holds the looming, leaning shadows. They fade as a match is struck. It flares in **SARAH**'*s hand, showing her face, and glimmers out against the wick of a dirty lantern. As the light of the lantern rises,* **J. B.** *is seen lying on the broken*

propped-up table, naked but for a few rags of clothing. **SARAH** *looks at him in the new light, shudders, lets her head drop into her hands. There is a long silence and then a movement in the darkness of the open door where four* **WOMEN** *and a young* **GIRL** *stand, their arms filled with blankets and newspapers. They come forward slowly into the light.*)[1]

NICKLES (*unseen, his cracked, cackling voice drifting down from the darkness of the platform overhead*).

Never fails! Never fails!
Count on you to make a mess of it!
Every blessed blundering time
You hit at one man you blast thousands.
Think of that Flood of yours—a massacre!
Now you've fumbled it again:
Tumbled a whole city down
To blister one man's skin with agony.[2]

(**NICKLES**' *white coat appears at the foot of the ladder. The* **WOMEN,** *in the circle of the lantern, are walking slowly around* **J. B.** *and* **SARAH,** *staring at them as though they were figures in a show window.*)[3]

NICKLES. Look at your works! Those shivering women
Sheltering under any crumbling
Heap to keep the sky out! Weeping![4]

MRS. ADAMS. That's him.

JOLLY ADAMS. Who's him?

MRS. ADAMS. Grammar, Jolly.

MRS. LESURE. Who did she say it was?[5]

MRS. MURPHY. Him she said it was.
Poor soul!

MRS. LESURE. Look at them sores on him!

MRS. ADAMS. Don't look, child.[6] You'll remember them.

JOLLY ADAMS (*proudly*). Every sore I seen I remember.

MRS. BOTTICELLI. Who did she say she said it was?

MRS. MURPHY. Him.

MRS. ADAMS. That's his wife.

MRS. LESURE. She's pretty.

MRS. BOTTICELLI. Ain't she.
Looks like somebody we've seen.

MRS. ADAMS (*snooting her*). I don't believe you would have seen her:

1. Note how the characters are systematically introduced. The timing of the opening, its choreography, is important for its emotional impact. How might music or sound effects be used to heighten the atmosphere of ruin and anguish?

2. Nickles helps set the scene. Which images receive the greatest emphasis?

3. Note the levels of action: J. B. and Sarah are at the center of the acting space, the women circle them, Nickles is a sort of dissociated voice encompassing the entire set. How do the tones and moods of the levels compare, contrast?

4. Who is weeping?

5. Remember that each of the women is a separate character and should have identifying mannerisms and vocal quality.

6. Be alert for textual hints for action.

Picture possibly—her picture
Posted in the penthouse.[7]

MRS. BOTTICELLI. Puce with pants?

MRS. ADAMS. No, the negligee.

MRS. BOTTICELLI. The net?

MRS. ADAMS. The simple silk.

Oh la! With sequins?[8]

MRS. MURPHY. Here's a place to park your poodle—
Nice cool floor.

MRS. LESURE. Shove over, dearie.

(*The* **WOMEN** *settle themselves on their newspapers off at the edge of the circle of light.* **NICKLES** *has perched himself on a chair at the side. Silence.*)[9]

J. B. (*a whisper*). God, let me die!

(**NICKLES** *leers up into the dark toward the unseen platform.*)

SARAH (her voice dead).[10] You think He'd help you
Even to that?

(*Silence.* **SARAH** *looks up, turning her face away from* **J. B.** *She speaks without passion, almost mechanically.*)

SARAH. God is our enemy.

J. B. No. . . . No. . . . No. . . . Don't
Say that Sarah!

(**SARAH'S** *head turns toward him slowly as though dragged against her will. She stares and cannot look away.*)

God had something
Hidden from our hearts to show.

NICKLES. She knows! She's looking at it![11]

J. B. Try to
sleep.

SARAH (*bitterly*). He should have kept it hidden.

J. B. Sleep now.

SARAH. You don't have to see it:
I do.[12]

J. B. Yes, I know.

NICKLES (*a cackle*). He knows!
He's back behind it and he knows!
If he could see what she can see
There's something else he might be knowing.

J. B. Once I knew a charm for sleeping—[13]
Not as forgetfulness but gift,
Not as sleep but second sight,

7. Why does Mrs. Adams repudiate Mrs. Botticelli?

8. Remember that the audience is aware of J. B. and Sarah as well as of the women. The difference in tone between these two levels creates tension. How might movement, gesture, and vocal quality be used here to attract the majority of attention to the women without completely overshadowing the sufferers?

9. What is the purpose of the silence? Practice for appropriate duration.

10. With what techniques might Sarah avoid monotony in affecting a dead voice?

11. If the three levels of characterization reflect various attitudes toward suffering (see note 3), what attitude does Nickles represent?

12. What is it which Sarah can see but which J. B. cannot?

13. Why does J. B. change the subject?

Come and from my eyelids lift
The dead of night.

SARAH. The dead . . .
of night . . .

(*She drops her head to her knees, whispering.*)
Come and from my eyelids lift
The dead of night.[14]

(*Silence.*)

J. B. Out of sleep
Something of our own comes back to us:
A drowned man's garment from the sea.

(**SARAH** *turns the lantern down. Silence. Then the voices of the* **WOMEN,** *low.*)[15]

MRS. BOTTICELLI. Poor thing!

MRS. MURPHY. Poor thing!
Not a chick not a child between them.

MRS. ADAMS. First their daughters. Then their sons.

MRS. MURPHY. First son first. Blew him to pieces.
More mischance it was than war.
Asleep on their feet in the frost they walked into it.

MRS. ADAMS. Two at the viaduct. That makes three.

JOLLY ADAMS (*a child's chant*). Jolly saw the picture! The picture!

MRS. ADAMS. Jolly Adams, you keep quiet.

JOLLY ADAMS. Wanna know? The whole of the viaduct. . . .

MRS. ADAMS. Never again will you look at them! Never!

MRS. LESURE.[16] Them magazines! They're awful! Which?

MRS. MURPHY. And after that the little one.

MRS. BOTTICELLI. Who in the
World are they talking about, the little one?
What are they talking?

MRS. LESURE. I don't know.
Somebody dogged by death it must be.

MRS. BOTTICELLI. Him it must be.

MRS. LESURE. Who's him

MRS. ADAMS. You know who.

MRS. MURPHY. You remember. . . .

MRS. ADAMS. Hush! The child!

MRS. MURPHY. Back of the lumberyard.

14. How would Sarah speak these lines differently than J. B.? In what ways does the meaning of the lines change?

15. In the following discussion among the women, what dramatic purpose is served by recalling the deaths of J. B.'s children? How can this purpose be emphasized?

16. Determine specifically who is speaking to whom in these speeches. How do the speakers relate to each other? How might staging help define the relationships? Remember that the characterizations of the women must be consistent throughout the scene.

MRS. LESURE. Oh! Him!

MRS. MURPHY. Who did you think it was—
Penthouse and negligees, daughters and dying?

MRS. BOTTICELLI. Him? That's him? The millionaire?

MRS. LESURE. Millionaires he buys like cabbages.

MRS. MURPHY. He couldn't buy cabbages now by the look of him:
The rags he's got on.

MRS. BOTTICELLI. Look at them sores!

MRS. MURPHY. All that's left him now is her.

MRS. BOTTICELLI. Still that's something—a good woman.

MRS. MURPHY. What good is a woman to him with that hide on him?—
Or he to her if you think of it.

MRS. ADAMS. Don't!

MRS. LESURE. Can you blame her?

17. Is Mrs. Murphy compassionate? Why or why not? What is the dramatic purpose for the women haggling?

MRS. MURPHY. I don't blame her.[17]
All I say is she's no comfort
She won't cuddle.

MRS. ADAMS. Really, Mrs. . . .

MRS. MURPHY. Murphy call me. What's got into you? . . .
Nothing recently I'd hazard.

MRS. ADAMS. You're not so young yourself, my woman.

MRS. MURPHY. Who's your woman? I was Murphy's.

MRS. LESURE. None of us are maids entirely.

MRS. MURPHY. Maids in mothballs some might be.

MRS. ADAMS. Who might?

MRS. MURPHY. You might.

MRS. ADAMS. You! you're . . . historical!

MRS. MURPHY. I never slept a night in history!

MRS. BOTTICELLI. *I* have. Oh, my mind goes back.

MRS. ADAMS. None of that! We have a child here!

(*Silence.*)

18. To whom is Mrs. Adams speaking? Why the silence?

How far back?[18]

MRS. BOTTICELLI. I often wonder.
Farther than the first but . . . where?

MRS. MURPHY. What do you care? It's lovely country.

(*Silence.*)

Roll a little nearer, dearie,

Me backside's froze.

MRS. LESURE. You smell of roses.

MRS. MURPHY. Neither do you but you're warm.

MRS. BOTTICELLI. Well,
Good night, ladies. Good night, ladies. . . .[19]

(*Silence. Out of the silence, felt rather than heard at first, a sound of sobbing, a muffled, monotonous sound like the heavy beat of a heart.*)

J. B. If you could only sleep a little
Now they're quiet, now they're still.[20]

SARAH (*her voice broken*). I try. But oh I close my eyes and . . .
Eyes are open there to meet me!

(*Silence. Then* **SARAH'S** *voice in an agony of bitterness.*)
My poor babies! Oh, my babies!

(**J. B.** *pulls himself up, sits huddled on his table in the feeble light of the lamp, his rags about him.*)

J. B. (*gently*). Go to sleep.

SARAH. Go! Go where?
If there were darkness I'd go there.
If there were night I'd lay me down in it.
God has shut the night against me.
God has set the dark alight
With horror blazing blind as day
When I go toward it . . .
close my eyes.

J. B.[21] I know. I know those waking eyes.
His will is everywhere against us—
Even in our sleep, our dreams. . . .

NICKLES (*a snort of laughter up toward the dark of the platform*). *Your* will, *his* peace!
Doesn't seem to grasp that, does he?
Give him another needling twinge
Between the withers and the works—
He'll understand you better.

J. B. If I
Knew. . . . If I knew why!

NICKLES. If he knew
Why he wouldn't be there. He'd be
Strangling, drowning, suffocating,
Diving for a sidewalk somewhere. . . .

19. How would the women be positioned when the focus returns to J. B.? How could a variety of stage levels enhance the final moments?

20. What does J. B. mean?

21. How would J. B.'s voice contrast with Sarah's?

J. B. What I *can't* bear is the blindness—
Meaninglessness—the numb blow
Fallen in the stumbling night.

SARAH (*starting violently to her feet*). Has death no meaning? Pain no meaning?

(*She points at his body.*)

Even these suppurating sores—
Have they no meaning for you?

NICKLES. Ah!

J.B. (*from his heart's pain*). God will not punish without cause.

(**NICKLES** *doubles up in spasms of soundless laughter.*)

J.B. God is just.

SARAH (*hysterically*). God is just!
If God is just our slaughtered children
Stank with sin, were rotten with it!

(*She controls herself with difficulty, turns toward him, reaches her arms out, lets them fall.*)

Oh, my dear! my dear! my dear!
Does God demand deception of us?—
Purchase His innocence by ours?
Must we be guilty for Him?—bear
The burden of the world's malevolence
For Him who made the world?

J.B. *He*
Knows the guilt is mine. He must know:
Has He not punished it? He knows its
Name, its time, its face, its circumstance,
The figure of its day, the door,
The opening of the door, the room, the moment. . . .

SARAH (*fiercely*). And you? Do you? You do not know it.
Your punishment is all you know.

22. What emotions motivate Sarah? How can her voice and movements help show her conflict?

(*She moves toward the door, stops, turns.*)[22]

I will not stay here if you lie—
Connive in your destruction, cringe to it:
Not if you betray my children . . .

I will not stay to listen. . . .

They are
Dead and they were innocent: I will not
Let you sacrifice their deaths

To make injustice justice and God good!

J.B. (*covering his face with his hands*). My heart beats. I cannot answer it.

SARAH. If you buy quiet with their innocence—
Theirs or yours . . .[23]

(*Softly.*)
I will not love you.

J.B. I have no choice but to be guilty.

SARAH (*her voice rising*). We have the choice to live or die,
All of us . . .
curse God and die. . . .

(*Silence.*)

J.B. God is God or we are nothing—
Mayflies that leave their husks behind—
Our tiny lives ridiculous—a suffering
Not even sad that Someone Somewhere
Laughs at as we laugh at apes.
We have no choice but to be guilty.
God is unthinkable if we are innocent.[24]

(**SARAH** *turns, runs soundlessly out of the circle of light, out of the door. The* **WOMEN** *stir.* **MRS. MURPHY** *comes up on her elbow.*)

MRS. MURPHY. What did I say? I said she'd walk out on him.

MRS. LESURE. She did.

MRS. BOTTICELLI. Did she?

MRS. MURPHY. His hide was too much for her.

MRS. BOTTICELLI. His hide or his heart.

MRS. MURPHY. The hide comes between.

MRS. BOTTICELLI. The heart is the stranger.

MRS. MURPHY. Oh, stranger!
It's always strange, the heart is: only
It's the skin we ever know.

J.B. (*raising his head*). Sarah, why do you not speak to me?
Sarah!

(*Silence.*)[25]

MRS. ADAMS. Now he knows.

MRS. MURPHY. And he's alone now.

23. Gestures and positions should be planned to heighten the intensity of this moment. Would Sarah remain motionless through her final pleas? Why or why not?

24. What is Sarah's facial expression? How does J. B. react to her exit?

25. What is the purpose of the silence? How might the vocal qualities of the women change? Would they still be unmoved as the scene closes? Why or why not? Would their actions be toward or away from J. B.? Why?

(**J.B.**'*s head falls forward onto his knees. Silence. Out of the silence his voice in an agony of prayer.*)

J.B. Show me my guilt, O God!

NICKLES. *His*
Guilt! His! You heard that didn't you?
He wants to feel the feel of guilt—
That putrid poultice of the soul
That draws the poison in, not out—
Inverted catheter! You going to show him?[26]

26. What gesture might be appropriate here?

(*Silence.* **NICKLES** *rises, moves toward the ladder.*)
Well? You going to show him . . . Jahveh?
(*Silence. He crosses to the ladder's foot.*)
Where are those cold comforters of yours
Who justify the ways of God to
Job by making Job responsible?—
Those three upholders of the world—
Defenders of the universe—where are they?
(*Silence. He starts up the ladder. Stops. The jeering tone is gone. His voice is bitter.*)
Must be almost time for comfort! . . .
(**NICKLES** *vanishes into the darkness above. The light fades.*)

Improvisation

J. B.

Cast. The cast sits in a circle. There are two parts to this game, the prologue and the play. For the prologue, one member sits in the center of the circle, eyes closed. A player at random from the circle rises and, while moving around the outer edge of the circle, speaks to the player in the center, improvising a few sentences which establish a relationship between them and reveal the speaker's feelings toward the player in the center. The speaker returns to the circle and sits down. This process is repeated by two more random players, each in turn improvising the details of a personal relationship to the player in the center.

For example, the first speaker might establish that he is the brother of the player in the center. He has just returned from two years in Viet Nam. He is clearly angry with her for not having written to him all that time. The second speaker might become her estranged husband and accuse her of being an unfit mother. The third, picking up on the previous improvisation, might establish that she is the daughter of the player in the center. She believes her mother does not want her, because she has been made to live with her grandmother (while her parents are wrangling over her custody). Her grandmother is mean to her, and she does not want to live with her father.

When the prologue has been accomplished in that manner, the play begins. The player in the center, her identity already established for her by the prologue, opens her eyes and stands. One at a time, each of the other three players returns to visit and improvises a scene with her which is based on the information presented in the prologue. While improvising these scenes, the object is to create a sequence, to tie together all the various relationships into a unified story, which is resolved when the last player leaves the playing area.

from

NOAH

ACT 1

Andre Obey
adapted by Arthur Wilmurt

The only speaker in this scene, the opening passage of the play, is the Biblical Noah. Generally, the scene is a soliloquy, though Noah addresses God and the various animals which appear. When the play begins, Noah is just finishing the ark which God had commissioned him to build. Since the interaction of the various animals is important to the effect of the scene, it is suggested that these parts be retained.

A central problem for the actor is that he is the scene's sole speaker. He will have to develop appropriate stage business and a variety of vocal and personal physical techniques which will help sustain the audience's interest. Vocal and physical techniques must help the audience follow Noah's shifting thoughts. His thoughts must seem spontaneous, following naturally, one from another. Vocal and physical techniques will also be important when Noah speaks to God. In a sense, the actor must create God's presence for the audience, for the audience neither sees nor hears God. Noah must give the impression that he is reacting directly with God, as though God were another character in the scene.

(*A glade. The Ark is at the Right, only the poop showing, with a ladder to the ground.* **NOAH** *is taking measurements and singing a little song. He scratches his head and goes over the measurements again. Then he calls.*)

NOAH (*softly*). Lord—(*Louder.*) Lord—(*Very loud.*) Lord. —Yes, Lord, it's me. Terribly sorry to bother you again, but—What? Yes, I know you've other things to think of, but after I've shoved off, won't it be a little late? Oh, no, Lord, no, no, no—Now, Lord, please don't think that—Oh, but look, of course I trust you! You could tell me to set sail on a plank—on a branch—on just a cabbage leaf. Why, you could tell me to put out to sea with nothing but my loincloth, even without my loincloth—completely—Yes, yes, I beg your pardon. Your time is precious. Well, this is all I wanted to ask: Should I make a rudder? I say, a rudder—No, no. R as in Robert; U as in Hubert; D as in—That's it, a rudder. Ah, good—very good, very good. The winds, the current, the tides—What was that, Lord? The tempests? Oh, and while I have you, one other little question—Are you listening, Lord? Gone! He's in a temper—Well, you can't blame Him; He has so much to think of. All right; no rudder. (*He considers the ark.*) The tides, the currents, the winds. (*He imitates the winds.*) Psch!—Psch!—The tempests. (*He imitates the tempests.*) Vloum! Ba da bloum!—That's going to be something—(*He makes a quick movement.*)—No, no, Lord, I'm not afraid. I know that you'll be with me. I was just trying to imagine—Oh, Lord, while you're there I'd like to ask—(*To the audience.*) Chk! Gone again. You see how careful you have to be. (*He laughs.*) He was listening all the time. Tempests—I'm going to put a few more nails in down here. (*He hammers and sings.*)

When the boat goes well, all goes well.
When all goes well, the boat goes well.

(*He admires his work.*) And when I think that a year ago I couldn't hammer a tack without mashing a nail. That's pretty good, if I do say so myself. (*He climbs aboard the ark and stands there like a captain.*) Larboard and starboard!—Cast off!—Close the portholes! —'Ware shoals!—Wait till the squall's over—Good!—Fine! Now I'm ready, completely ready, super-ready! (*He cries to heaven.*) I am ready! (*Then quietly.*) There. I'd like to know how this business is going to begin. (*He looks all around, at the trees, the bushes, and the sky.*) The weather is magnificent; the heat—oppressive, and there's not a sign of a cloud. Well, that part of the program is His affair. (*Enter the* **BEAR** *Left.*) Well!—Now what does *he* want? (**BEAR** *moves toward the ark*)

Just a minute there! (**BEAR** *makes a pass at the ark.* **NOAH** *frightened.*) Stop it! (**BEAR** *stops.*) Good. Sit down! (**BEAR** *sits.*) Lie down. (**BEAR** *lies down on its back and waves its legs gently.*) There, that's a good doggie. (*Enter the* **LION** *Left.*) What the devil! (**LION** *puts its paw on the ark.*) Stop that, you!—And lie down. (**LION** *lies down beside the* **BEAR.**) Fine!—Splendid!—Now what do they want? And besides, why don't they fight? (*To the* **ANIMALS.**) Hey! Why aren't you fighting? Come on, there. Boo! Woof! (*The* **BEAR** *and the* **LION** *get up and sniff at each other sociably.*) Who ever heard of wild animals acting like that? (*Enter the* **MONKEY** *Left.*) Another one!—It's a zoo—Sit down, you monkey. Now, look here, my pets, for a year I've been working here every day. Not one of you has ever shown me the tip of his nose. Now that I've finished, are you out to make trouble for me? Go on, this doesn't concern you. (*He thinks it over.*) Unless—But then, that changes everything—Lord! Lord! (*Between his teeth.*) Naturally He isn't there! (*Enter the* **ELEPHANT** *Left.*) Get back there, Jumbo! (**ELEPHANT** *salutes him.*) Good morning, my fine fellow. Now, if I understand you, you want to get aboard, eh? (*The* **ANIMALS** *move forward.*) Stop! I didn't say you could!—Good. All right, I'll let you come aboard—Yes, I don't see what I can—No, I don't see anything against it. (*He sighs deeply.*) So the time has come! All right. Up with you! (*Enter the* **COW,** *Left, gamboling.*) Gently there, gently—And get in the rear. (*He taps* **COW** *on the rump.*) But wait a minute. Don't I know you? Aren't you that old cow from Mardocheus's herd? (**COW** *moos gaily.*) For heaven's sake! (*With feeling.*) And He's chosen you! (*To the* **BEAR.**) Well, my friend, will you make up your mind? (**BEAR** *sniffs the ground, but doesn't advance.*) What's the matter, old boy? (**NOAH** *puts on his spectacles and leans over the spot where the* **BEAR** *is sniffing.*) What? You're afraid of that insect? An ant! Ha, ha, ha! A bear afraid of an ant. Ha, ha, ha! (*But suddenly he strikes his brow.*) But what a fool I am! That's not an ant, it's *the* ant! It got here first, and I never saw it. Lord! What marvels there are on the threshold of this new life.

It will take a stout heart, a steady hand, and a clear eye! I think my heart is right, but my eyes are dim—my hand is trembling—my feet are heavy—Ah, well, if You've chosen me, perhaps it's because I am like her—the least wicked of the herd. Come, all aboard. Make yourselves at home. (*The* **ANIMALS** *go into the ark.*) Straight ahead, across the deck. Down the stairway to your left. You'll find your cabins ready. They may look like cages, but they'll be open always. (*He turns towards the forest Left.*) Come one, come all! Hurry, you lazy ones, you slow-pokes, you crawlers, you who travel in droves and you who live alone, forked hoofs, hunchbacks! Hurry! Everyone! Everyone! (*He catches his breath.*) Ah ha! Here comes the wolf and the lamb, side by side. (*The* **WOLF** *and the* **LAMB** *enter Left and go into the ark.*) Here is the bullfrog and the bull—The fox and the raven. And the birds! What are they waiting for? Come, my little ones. Come! Come! (*The singing of the* **BIRDS** *begins.*) Look. The hare and the tortoise! Come on. Come on. Hurrah! The hare wins! Things are getting back to normal! Ah, this will be the golden age!

Improvisation

NOAH

Noah. You are Noah. You operate a small, not very profitable soy bean farm in the Midwest. The news media have gotten wind of your alleged conversations with God, and a TV camera crew has arrived at your home. Improvise a scene in which you are being interviewed by remote control from the main studios of a national network by a dubious, unseen anchor man. Of course, your improvisation will really be a monlogue, in which you must imagine the interviewer's questions. Examples of the kind of questions you might respond to are: when did God first contact you, and what were you doing at the time; why do you think God is picking on you of all people; what do your neighbors think about your ark; is it true that your wife and children think you are crazy; how do you feel about most of the rest of the nation doubting your word; and what about the TV weathermen who dispute your prediction of a deluge?

Noah, Animals. Imagine that you (Noah) have at last convinced your irritable wife to come and take a look at the ark you have been building. Improvise a scene in which you describe the ark to your (imaginary) wife as you show her its various decks, compartments, and so forth, and introduce her to the various animals located here and there all over the structure. Use as much space and as many levels as you need to acquaint her with what is to be her new home. (Those of you playing the animals will want to study the ways in which the movements and "personalities" of real animals differ from each other. To convincingly portray a specific animal, without the aid of a costume, is a real challenge.)

ABOUT THE AUTHOR

Before joining the faculty of California State University, San Francisco, Dr. Elkind taught drama at El Cerrito High School, El Cerrito, California. He had been president of the California Educational Theatre Association, Governor of the Secondary School Theatre Association, Director of the High School Drama Workshop at California State University, San Francisco, and Consultant to the State Department of Education for California. Articles by Dr. Elkind have appeared in *Dramatics, The Speech Teacher, The Secondary School Theatre and the CTA Journal*. He is the coauthor of *Drama/Theatre Framework for California Public Schools*. Besides *Improvisation, Theatre Games and Scene Handbook*, Dr. Elkind is the author of *Scenes for Acting and Directing Vol. 1*, *Scenes for Acting and Directing Vol. 2* and *Scenes for Acting and Directing Vol. 3*.

In addition to his wide service in the California school system, Dr. Elkind was a professional director for theater groups in the San Francisco Bay Area. He also produced, directed, and moderated discussion and panel programs for local television and radio.